The Newcomer

Red Ridge Chronicles Book 6

Sarah Lamb

This is a work of fiction. Names, characters, businesses, places, events, locales, and incidents are either the products of the author's imagination or used in a fictitious manner. Any resemblance to actual persons, living or dead, or actual events is purely coincidental.

A thank you to my proofreader, Brooke, and all of the lovely women who help ARC read to catch those typos I miss!

This book was not written by AI. Any typos are proudly (and embarrassingly!) my own human created ones!

Paperback ISBN: 978-1-960418-63-0

Large print ISBN: 978-1-960418-64-7

Contents

To each of the special people who have helped me bring this series and many of my other books to life: Brooke, for her on-point suggestions and proofreading; Nancy, for her fantastic covers; Spencer, for his incredible narration; and you, dear readers, for your endless support.

Chapter 1

1870s Red Ridge, Oregon

Kent Jackson tried not to swagger as he walked through the hotel. His hotel now. Pride was nearly bursting out of him and it was hard to contain it. He took a deep breath and moved his arms behind his back, slowing his stride. There, that looked more professional.

Owner of a hotel... Kent had never imagined such a thing. It had just been by chance that he'd come through the town of Red Ridge a few months ago and stayed a night when the stagecoach broke down. It was then he'd learned that the couple who owned the hotel were ready to retire. Jokingly, the old man had offered to sell it to him.

With a laugh, Kent had replied he'd think about it. But even though he'd planned to dismiss the idea, he couldn't seem to stop thinking about the man's words.

Owning a hotel. The idea was oddly appealing. It wasn't something he'd ever considered before, but it could be a chance to make a secure future for himself. Stop going from place to place.

That pleased feeling surged through Kent again as he remembered how he'd approached the old hotel owner the next morning, and asked if he was serious about selling. It seemed everything happened quickly after that. Kent had returned a few days later after he'd arranged his finances. A few weeks after that, the hotel was his.

The couple had stayed on just long enough to explain how they'd done things and introduce him to their existing staff. They were eager to move to California, where their daughter lived, and gave their address in case he had more questions.

So far, all had gone well. Kent hadn't changed too much at first. But as he'd grown more confident in his abilities over the last few weeks, he'd made sure the rooms were updated, as were the staff uniforms and the restaurant menu.

He wanted to make this place feel like home, not just for himself, but for anyone passing through. That's why the rooms were clean and cozy, well-furnished but not ostentatious. The restaurant menu had just good plain home cooking. It seemed that those who visited always made mention on their way out they'd return. That made

Kent smile. Why, if this hotel became a success, he could even expand one day! Open two! Or three!

Now, as he took a slow look around at all he'd accomplished, Kent nodded with satisfaction. It felt good, owning something like this place. Getting his fresh start.

"Oh! Excuse me, Mr. Jackson." A hotel maid narrowly avoided running into him as she exited a room. Her crisp navy-colored dress with a white apron overtop looked professional. The woman gave him a brisk nod as she headed to the room across the hallway to clean, her duster in one hand.

Kent peered into the room she'd just finished cleaning, then stopped to straighten a painting with yellow flowers in it. Each of the rooms in the hotel was nearly identical. There were six rooms on the upper level, and three suites on the lower. He'd decided in addition to giving each a number, they'd also have a color theme. This was the yellow room. Tastefully done, a yellow bedspread, yellow curtains, and other yellow accents made the dark wood appear cozy, welcoming.

He walked through the rest of the room, but everything looked perfect. The maids—the hotel had three, plus the housekeeper who was in charge—were well trained and did their jobs exceedingly well. He couldn't have asked for better.

"Mr. Jackson?"

He turned, and saw the maid who'd passed him a moment before. "Yes, Laura?"

She held out a small pouch. "A guest must have left this behind. It was in the blue room, just under the desk chair."

"Ah, thank you," Kent said, taking it. "I'll ask Clyde to put it in the lost and found, along with a note of where you found it."

Laura nodded, and returned to the room, where Kent saw her remove the soiled linens, dropping them on the floor in a heap, and then shake out the fresh ones to put on. She was an honest worker. All of his staff were.

Kent looked down at the small pouch. Best to take that to Clyde now before he got distracted with some other task and forgot. The guest might return at any moment. He could inspect the rest of the upstairs later.

Clyde was the front desk manager. A man in his fifties, he'd worked for the hotel over a dozen years now, and was quite indispensable. Kent felt fortunate that the housekeeper and the restaurant chef were also long-time employees, and were both agreeable people. There hadn't been any sort of discontent when he took over. Instead, each had explained their jobs and how things had worked up until he'd bought the place, and answered whatever questions he had.

Kent headed toward the hall and to the staircase. The old oak floorboards nearly gleamed from a recent polishing. He made his way down the stairs, noting the squeak on the third one, and stepped into the hotel lobby.

It was a spacious area and decorated simply in navy. Directly in front of him were the wide double doors of the entrance. If one walked into the hotel, to the right was another set of doors that led to the restaurant. Inside, it could seat fifty. If, instead, a guest had walked straight, they'd see a small grouping of chairs and a table to the left, and before them the large check-in desk.

The hotel also boasted a garden with several benches and a small collection of rose bushes. Kent hoped to expand that slightly. If possible, he envisioned a lovely walking path with a fountain in the middle. The perfect place for guests to wander, and perhaps have an outdoor tea.

As Kent approached the front desk, the pouch in his hand jingled slightly. He swallowed hard as the sound brought him back to some moments in his life he wasn't proud of. Times when he'd made a lot of mistakes.

He was desperate to forget about his past. How tempting it was to just slip the little pouch into his pocket and pretend he knew nothing about it. How easy it would be. Kent had done it more times than he could count. But he did know about it, the money wasn't his, and the heaviness of the small bag was nothing compared to the heaviness in his soul at his past mistakes.

Red Ridge and this hotel were a fresh start. A chance to leave the past behind. But what he hadn't realized was that once you'd done something you weren't proud of, it was impossible to forget about it. Every day, in small ways, you were reminded of the wrong you'd done.

"Clyde, the guest in Room 3, our blue room, left this behind," Kent said, handing the manager the pouch.

"I'll mark that down, sir," Clyde said, taking the pouch after reaching into his navy pants pocket for a key, and heading for the back room where they kept a locked closet with any items that had been left behind.

Kent leaned against the desk, letting his gaze wander while he watched over the hotel front until Clyde returned. His eyes landed on the building almost directly across from him. The sheriff's office.

And there it was, just another reminder that at any moment, someone might find out who he was. It didn't matter that he had taken every penny he'd ever stolen and still had and given it to the church. Didn't even matter that he'd been honest for four years now, and every cent of buying this place he'd earned through hard work. First as a handyman, then as a stagecoach driver before getting the offer to own the place. Inside of him, a small voice whispered, *Who are you kidding? Once a liar and a thief, always one.*

Kent pulled his eyes from the sheriff's office and let them drift once more through the parts of town he could see.

This time, they landed on the smaller of the two general stores. His heart sped up as a figure passed the window, and he strained his eyes to see her better.

A small smile fought its way to his lips. Betty Doyle. He hadn't talked to her much, only now and again in her aunt's store, but he liked her. Could more than like her. But the dark cloud of doubt and guilt washed over him again. How could someone as innocent and sweet as Betty be friends or anything more—let alone anything at all—with a man like him? That was another thing he'd had no idea about. How once you were branded as he was, you were destined to spend your life alone.

Chapter 2

"Betty!" her aunt called from behind the general store counter. "I'm going upstairs to check on the stew."

"All right, Aunt Glinda," Betty Doyle answered, from where she was refolding the bolts of fabric that a customer had accidentally knocked over earlier that day.

As her aunt disappeared, Betty took a quick glance around the store to be sure no customer had snuck in when she was distracted. No, thankfully the store was empty just now. With a bit of luck, she'd get this display back in order. Often, there was an endless trickle of customers, and it made staying on top of the merchandise displays a little difficult.

Even though her aunt owned the second, and the smaller, general store in Red Ridge, she had numerous customers who came to her. The town was able to support both stores well, and her aunt focused more on items women would want and need, alongside her dry goods and tinned foods.

Like the fabric. No one else in town, except perhaps the dressmaker, had as much fabric as they did. There was also a large collection of lotions and soaps, of books, journals, pens and pencils, and sweets.

Betty spied a spool of thread under the table that also must have been knocked over and stooped down to get it. As she placed it back where it belonged, she felt a sense of satisfaction at the orderly way this section of the store looked, and decided to straighten up another area while the store was still empty.

It was a good distraction. By staying busy, she didn't have time to grieve the life she thought she'd have.

Though she'd only lived with her aunt for a few months, Betty was enjoying each moment of the routine. Though a recent letter from her parents called her job simple, running the shop was anything but.

It was quite a juggling act at moments, weighing goods and ringing up customers and waiting on several at once. She'd quickly learned who was patient and who was fussy, and how they each liked their orders bundled up.

The change had been good. Betty felt as though she was positively thriving here. She wasn't wasted, wasn't relegated to sitting in a corner quietly, where nothing ever happened. Wasn't sitting, fighting back tears and feeling unwanted.

Even if it was just minding the shop, she was needed by someone. Could fuss about, and make things better. It was different from being back home, where her days felt mind-numbing, as she simply sewed or sipped tea, gardened with her mother and sister, or sat around making polite and dull conversation.

Here, she was enjoying feeling a part of the town. Her aunt's business was a cornerstone of the community. People gathered here not just for supplies but also news and gossip. Betty enjoyed the bustle within the store, and it was just what she needed too, to help her heal. Each day that passed, she felt a little lighter. A little happier.

When the letter from her aunt had first arrived, asking if she might want to assist for a short time, it was all Betty could do not to pack and leave the same day. Truthfully, had she known how much she'd have enjoyed being here, maybe she'd have come sooner!

It had taken a little convincing to get her parents to agree to let her assist Aunt Glinda. They had been worried she was going to be subjected to rough ways and grow even more independent than she already seemed. To Betty, that was ridiculous. After all, she'd had the same upbringing in social graces as her sister. Could she help it, though, if she were twenty-six, and unmarried? Some independence was called for at this advanced age! If marriage wasn't to be in her future, she needed to do something to support herself.

After all, she wasn't going to be quick about giving her heart away again, not after the hurt she'd experienced.

Thankfully, after another letter exchange with her aunt, and hearing about how men vastly outnumbered women in the West, her parents' fears vanished, fast replaced with the idea that perhaps the ideal beau was there in the form of a wealthy rancher or a man who'd struck gold, and Betty was given permission to leave. Her younger sister hadn't even really noticed her departure; she was too enamored by her upcoming nuptials.

Nuptials that should have been Betty's.

Betty paused in front of the large glass window overlooking the street and studied her reflection. Just before she'd left home, her mother had made Betty promise to try to attract the attention of local eligible bachelors.

"Don't appear too smart," she'd told Betty. "But don't seem too desperate, either. If there are comments about how old you are and how you aren't married yet, say something like...you've spent your years being dutiful, helping your parents."

Dutiful. Yes, that was something Betty had always been, even if she felt sure she could be more, wanted to experience more, and wished she'd have a chance to be. Perhaps that was why she enjoyed the shop and her aunt's company so much. Aunt Glinda recognized her aptitude for running the store, and so far had been nothing but complimentary. It kept her mind off of the fact she was sorely lacking, in her parents' minds.

Was that enough, however? Her mother would say no. She was plain, but attractive enough, she supposed, if that was important to a man. But the things she did have to offer—such as her quick ability to work sums in her mind, her new instinct for creating eye-catching displays, and ideas for drawing in more customers wasn't exactly suitable for the kind of thing she might need to attract a mate. How would any of the shopkeeping skills be useful? After all, that's how she'd ended up being hurt, wasn't it? She'd been...too much, and somehow, not enough at all.

Her mother's voice rang around in her head, almost burning her ears. "Betty! Do better! Can't you be more like your sister?"

Now, that was a phrase she'd heard often. Be more pleasing. Be more friendly. Be more shy. Be more quiet. Be less clever. All of those be's, and each of them followed with the words, like your sister.

Back home, Betty had been told being too clever was a downfall, not an asset. That while working sums would be useful for her household budget, she should focus more on her needlework and cooking skills, things that would be desirable to a husband. How men didn't appreciate women who tried to be too assertive or overstep their place.

Though Betty wasn't completely sure that was honestly the case, she also hadn't tried to argue. When you argued with your mother, you never won.

Betty hadn't spoken to her aunt about her worry, though she felt sure Aunt Glinda would listen. It's just that she didn't feel it would be appropriate, especially as her aunt was a widow and a shop owner. Aunt Glinda did a wonderful job of being independent.

Also, her aunt had been married once, but lost her husband shortly after she'd wedded. She'd raised a child on her own, run the store on her own, and hadn't shown any interest in remarriage, so how would she understand? While her aunt might be a listening ear, she wouldn't be a source of experience to help her.

Betty's gaze drifted to the street, where she saw her new friend Callie walking along with her intended, a tracker named Ryan Lundy, and friend to the gunslingers who kept the town safe.

A small sigh escaped as she watched Ryan kiss Callie goodbye as he went into the sheriff's office, and she walked to the dressmaker. For all of her happiness at being here, being an independent woman, and away from her parents' nagging about finding an intended, the fact was that she did want one. Her heart still felt broken at times.

Perhaps one day she would have a love of her own. Someone to make her heart flutter, and butterflies to form up and soar within her. Someone who wouldn't ignore her.

Her thoughts wandered back to her sister again. That's just how her sister said love felt. Betty knew it was true, even if she couldn't admit it. The secret burned within her, a mixture of sorrow and shame. It swelled up each time she thought about her sister.

Her perfect, lovely sister. Betty's sister was the one to catch the eye of all who saw her. With soft curls in her hair, and a sweet face with wide eyes and pouty lips, she was a stark contrast to Betty's straight hair, sharp eyes, and thinner lips that found themselves all too often pressing together. But that was how she held back the things she felt. The things she longed to say. Things that didn't matter, not when she wasn't wanted.

Betty was tired of not being wanted. Of being passed over. And here, in Oregon, at least she wouldn't have to feel that way each time she saw her sister and her sister's intended. She could have a fresh start, reinvent herself if she wished.

At least, that's what the newspaper she'd picked up for the long stagecoach ride had suggested. *The West is for Reinvention!* the article had proclaimed. And that's just what she was trying to experience. Who knew? Betty thought she might enjoy living here permanently. After she'd been here for a while, perhaps she could tell her aunt she'd like the opportunity to stay, to make Red Ridge and the store her home, with the intention of running it herself one day.

The shop door opened, and a soft bell jingled. Betty quickly turned, and then tried not to stammer when she saw who it was. "Hello, Mr. Jackson," she told the hotel owner.

She squeezed her hands together, hoping he wouldn't see how nervous she felt talking to him. For some reason, there was something about him that made her feel self-conscious. Off kilter. And think about him long after he'd left.

Which was ridiculous, and highly inappropriate. The man had been nothing but polite, and she had no reason to believe he'd ever be anything more than that, especially to someone as simple as she was. He'd arrived a short time before her, but had quickly settled in and found his place with an ease she admired.

"Kent," he corrected her with a broad smile as he walked closer. "I've told you that. That's also why you told me I could call you Betty."

How she loved when he used her name.

"So you have," she answered, with a shy blush. "I'm sorry. A habit, I suppose, of greeting customers that way."

"Nothing to be sorry for," he answered. "I do the same when someone comes into my hotel."

There was a moment of awkward silence, then Betty asked, "Is that a list in your hand?"

"Yes," Kent said, looking down at the sheet of paper. "I've a few things I need, and others I'd like to place an order for."

"Let me see what we have on here," Betty offered, reaching toward the list.

Their fingers brushed, and the warm tingles she adored each time she took his list or handed over a parcel to him worked their way shivering up her arm. He came in at least twice a week, though Betty wished it were every day.

She scanned the list, then shook her head. "We will have to order all of this, I'm afraid. I can send off the order today though, and you'll have it soon."

"That's fine," he said. "Whenever you can get it is appreciated."

Betty tried not to let her shoulders slump in disappointment as she heard her aunt's soft footsteps signaling her return. Not a moment later, she took her spot behind the counter, while Betty stepped to the side slightly to make room.

"How are you?" her aunt greeted, and then looked over Betty's shoulder at the list. "Hmm. This all must be ordered."

"That's no problem at all. Thank you," Kent said. "I'm afraid I must be going. But I'll stop in soon."

He held up a hand in farewell, and Betty couldn't help herself. She watched as he left, and hoped she was able to hide any sort of expression beyond one of politeness.

Once the door had closed, her aunt made a humming sound, and Betty looked over to see her frowning as she watched Kent walking toward the hotel. "Something about that man," her aunt said. "I'm just not sure I trust him. I almost wish he wouldn't do his shopping here."

"What do you mean?" Betty asked.

"I don't know," her aunt mused, giving a small shrug. "Just...he seems like he's got secrets."

"Many people do," Betty said lightly, as she pulled out the order form booklet. "But you know as well as I do, the sheriff and his gunslinger friends won't let anything happen to this town. They've protected it many times."

"True," her aunt said. "And his large orders for the hotel are appreciated. Perhaps I'm just a suspicious old woman, wary of newcomers. It's still not a habit not to watch my back in this town, after all the trouble we had with the crooked sheriff and the people he let do whatever they wanted."

Betty shivered. She'd heard some of the stories, and was glad she hadn't been here then. "I bet the sheriff has had his eye on him since he arrived," she tried to reassure her aunt. "Any trouble, I suspect they'll run him out."

The door opened just then and Callie walked in with a smile.

"How are you?" Betty greeted her.

"Wonderful," Callie said eagerly as she approached. "I just finished writing my most recent story. I need some new blank books, though. This afternoon, I'm going to start writing Winnie and Gavin's story."

"How exciting!" Betty said. "When do I get to read the one you just finished? Now that I'm all caught up on what happened with Hannah and Eli, I want to read about Mirabelle and Billy."

"Soon, I hope," Callie said, as she walked to the selection of blank books and picked one up. "It turns out that Aiden—you know, Dr. Rycroft, Nora's husband?—has a friend who is a publisher. He's encouraging me to send my stories to him, and promises he'll enclose a note to improve my chances of it getting read. Though," she laughed, "he's asked I be sure his part in their story is quite heroic."

"How could it be anything but?" Betty asked, crossing her arms over her chest. "Aunt Glinda said he was largely responsible for saving the entire town when the sickness swept through. Why, he—"

She paused and bit her lip then. Maybe she shouldn't have said anything. After all, Callie had lost her first husband during the sickness, and though later she'd admitted he'd been a horrible man, Betty worried that any sort of reminder might bring those moments back to her friend. She didn't want to cause her any pain.

"I know what you're thinking," her friend said with a kind smile. "I'm quite fortunate, and even blessed, with how things turned out. And I quite agree. He is a hero, and he and Nora are so suited."

She set two books on the counter, and asked, "Could I also please have three pencils? No, make that four."

"Here you are, dear," Aunt Glinda said, and wrapped everything in brown paper. Once done, she added a thick white string around it, busily tying it in a bow. "I placed an order too, last week, for more blank books. I asked for an assortment of colors, in the size that you like best."

"Oh! How wonderful. Then I will stop in again soon to see them," Callie said.

She reached into her handbag, paid for her items, and as she walked away, Betty wondered to herself. If a story were written about her, what would it be? Filled with the heartache she suffered? Perhaps. Did she even have anything else interesting that happened in her life to fill the pages of a book? It was doubtful.

One thing was for sure. No happy ending was likely to be in store for her. Not when her sister was going to marry the man she had wanted and her parents thought her worthless.

Chapter 3

The hotel restaurant still buzzed in quiet whispers, but it was starting to settle. Kent hoped the throbbing in his head would soon settle too. He hadn't realized something like this might happen in his establishment.

He also hadn't realized just how nervous he'd feel, standing so close to the sheriff, who seemed to have a way of looking at everything and everyone at once. It was most unsettling.

"I appreciate you coming so quickly," Kent said to Sheriff Gavin Jefferson. He wiped at his brow. "That man got very agitated very quickly."

"It happens," the sheriff said, turning his attention back to Kent, "but I think he understands now that kind of behavior isn't allowed here. Not in your hotel and not in town."

"I hope so," Kent said with a frown. The sheriff had strongly suggested the man who'd been causing the ruckus in the restaurant leave on the early stage, and said he'd be there to ensure it.

It had been a quiet evening, until the man had smacked one of the waitresses on her backside. When she'd asked him to stop, he did it again, which resulted in the woman giving him a smack of her own. The guest had been so angry, he'd overturned the table and chased after her.

It had taken half of the diners and the manager and himself to restrain the man, who'd been acting with surprising strength. Luckily, someone had run for the sheriff, and he'd arrived quickly, putting a stop to the whole escapade.

Kent turned and planned to make another round in the restaurant, assuring everyone that all was well, and make amends if needed. He'd already promised there would be no charge for the diners that evening, and that included the desserts that he'd told the chef to get ready to send out on the house.

As for the waitress, he'd assured her she wasn't in any trouble, nor in fear of losing her job. He'd offered to let her have the evening off, but she'd squared her shoulders, muttered something about not letting anyone run her off, and headed back out into the dining room.

What an evening. Still, if this was the most difficult thing he had to deal with, the occasional rowdy guest, he'd consider himself lucky. As Kent turned to make his rounds through the remaining guests who were dining, a smile and ready apology on his lips, a voice stopped him cold.

"You aren't planning to call the sheriff on us now, are you?"

Every fiber in his being tensed, and it was all Kent could do to suppress a shiver. He knew that voice. It still tormented him in his darkest moments. Why was he here? But, just as quickly, he thought how foolish he'd been, thinking that he'd be able to get away. Escape. Leave his past behind. He'd been so careful, but he should have known better. Eventually, the past catches up, and the piper must be paid.

Turning, Kent forced a smile on his face. The surprise wasn't something he had to feign. "Harry! Wait! And Jimbo? Am I seeing right?"

"That's right, you old son of a gun," Harry said, slapping him on the shoulder. For a man about six inches shorter than him, he was quite strong, and Kent rocked backward from the wider man's forceful attention. Harry squinted at him and gave a slow shake of the head. "I thought Wildey was fooling when he said he'd heard you set up shop here."

"I haven't set up shop," Kent said, hoping his former acquaintances would keep their voices down. "I own the hotel."

"That's what he told us," Jimbo said, and gazed around the lobby. "You'll be putting us up."

It wasn't a question. Kent swallowed, and nodded briskly. "Of course I will be. How long are you boys staying?"

"Long as it takes," Jimbo grunted.

"Now look," Kent said, hoping his tone was one of friendly concern, "I don't want any trouble. You ought to know, the sheriff is a pretty mindful fellow. Former gunslinger, and he and his friends keep close watch on the town. If you're planning something—"

"'Course not!" Harry said, smacking his shoulder again. "We're just here to relax. A little rest for the weary." He glared at Jimbo. "Ain't that right?"

"What he said," Jimbo answered. He sniffed the air. "Where's the grub?"

"Ah, the dining room just had an upset," Kent said, "so we've stopped taking customers for the night. How about I give you our best room, a suite, and have the meal sent there?"

"Sounds fancy like," Harry said. "I approve. I am a mite tired."

"Yeah. Better to take in the town when there's not so many people around," Jimbo agreed.

"Now look—" Kent said.

"You've got nothing to worry about." Harry gave him a grin, and Kent noticed the man had fewer teeth than the last time he'd seen him, which was when they were riding alongside a stagecoach, bandanas over their faces, guns pulled out and pointing to get it to stop.

"I'm going to hold you to that," Kent said grimly. He added, hoping his voice sounded lighter, "Like I said, the sheriff keeps a real close eye on things. That's why I've gone straight."

"Sure, sure," Jimbo said with a guffaw. "You may say it, but can't never do that. Not a man like you. Perfect set up you got here. Rich folks coming and going. Brilliant."

Kent didn't answer. Couldn't. What would he say? Nothing could convince either of the men of the truth. The fact was, one day, Kent had woken up and realized that the things he'd been doing weren't the kind of things he wanted to do anymore.

When he thought back over it, he wasn't even sure how he'd gotten mixed up with Harry and Jimbo. Must have been just plain old desperation. Too many nights of sleeping with a gnawing belly. The tired feeling of being looked down on by those who thought they were better than him. Maybe it was just the simple allure, the thought that a few dollars in his pocket would buy respectability. Freedom. Comfort.

The temptation of an easy life caused a man to do things he didn't want to do, and over time, those things, along with hanging around people like Harry and Jimbo, became habits, and then a way of life.

He'd wanted to stop, though. Before it was too late for him. A tightness filled his chest. He had to get them out of town as fast as possible. Before he grew weak, or got in trouble. It was dangerous, the two of them being here. Being a business owner meant a responsibility to the town. He couldn't let Harry and Jimbo bother the town or anyone in it.

And he couldn't let them tempt him.

Kent walked to the check-in desk, and gave Clyde a tight smile. "Key two, please."

"Sir," Clyde said, handing it to him.

Though the manager's face was neutral, Kent could see a little curiosity, especially when Kent didn't have them sign the guest register. "Old friends," Kent said, then, his voice low, added, "former friends. But I want to keep them happy. Whatever they need, on me."

"I understand, sir," Clyde said, and somehow Kent suspected he did. He appreciated how there was no judgment in the other man's face. Sometimes, they all had to do something they might not like to survive.

Kent held the key up as he turned back to Harry and Jimbo. "If you'll follow me?"

He led them down the hallway, and to the suite that was the furthest away. Hopefully, the two wouldn't be noisy, but if they were, they were more isolated from the other guests. As much as possible, he wanted to keep them in their room.

"Remember," Kent warned, as he unlocked the door and handed Harry the key.

"We know, we know," Harry said, walking in the room and setting down the bag he'd been carrying. "No trouble."

Kent nodded, and left, closing the door behind him. He wished he could believe them, but he wasn't sure he could. Maybe they'd figure out for themselves that Red Ridge didn't hold anything for them.

Or maybe he'd be the one who was run out, only at the end of a gunslinger's barrel.

Chapter 4

"Welcome," Betty called, and then turned around from where she'd been stacking some tins with a specialty tea blend.

"Howdy. Ah, Glinda around?" Gus stood, shuffling his feet, his weathered face looking a little sheepish. "Thought I'd get me some peppermints, and she knows just how I like them. No offense to you," Gus said, winking at her. "She's just got a right special way about things."

"Let me get her," Betty said, hiding her smile. There was no way at all he'd gone through all of the peppermints he'd bought the day before, or the day before that. Perhaps her aunt could convince him to go for the lemon drops. Those had been selling slower as of late.

"Can I see that tea you got there?" Gus asked. "Reckon I might get some of that too. Hannah enjoys an afternoon cup."

"Of course. It seems everyone in town is enjoying it," Betty said, setting the container on the counter.

After discovering the blend in a catalog, Betty had suggested her aunt stock it, in addition to the regular tea she always sold, just to see how it was and to offer something different to her customers. To their surprise, the tea flew off the shelves and they could hardly keep it in stock.

It had been such a success, and made such a tidy sum in profits, that her aunt had encouraged her to make more suggestions for the store's inventory. Something Betty planned to do. After all, any success would keep her aunt's shop busier, and that would mean that Betty would have to stay to help her! She wasn't eager to go home, and she was enjoying her time here in the store. It kept her mind busy, and that was something she enjoyed. Not to mention, there was Kent.

Betty left from behind the counter, and headed to the back of the store. "Aunt Glinda?" Betty called as she moved closer to the storeroom.

"I'm here," her aunt said, and climbed off the small step ladder she'd been using.

"Gus is here," Betty said.

She didn't need to say another word. Her aunt flushed as brightly as a young girl might at the mention and smoothed her dress. "Is that so? Did he need a little help?"

"He does," Betty said. Then, she decided to give them a little time to talk. "Since part of the hotel's spice order is in, would you mind if I took it to them? I'd love to step into the sunshine for a little, and I'm sure their cook needs it."

"Go ahead," her aunt said, as she walked to the storefront.

Betty nodded, and picked up the small crate marked for the hotel. Since the full order hadn't arrived, it would be easy to take this over. Maybe she'd see Kent on the way. She tried to fight back her own blush at the idea, and gave a soft laugh. She was as bad as her aunt. The two of them interested in a man. The only difference was Gus seemed to return that interest, and Betty didn't think Kent was anything more than friendly.

Voices drifted down the hallway, as well as a giggle. Betty smiled in the direction, happy for her aunt, as she slipped out the back door. It was obvious to her, and likely everyone else in town, that her aunt and Gus liked each other. The question they all had, though, was would anything come of it? Would the two of them ever admit to themselves there was something a little more than friendly conversation brewing?

Betty tipped her head upward, letting the warm sun beat down on her. It was only a short walk to the hotel, so lingering would look silly, but she still walked slowly. She could see Eli Jones sitting in front of the sheriff's office, reading something. He looked up and nodded at her, and she did the same in reply.

Though she'd never spoken to him much, she knew his wife, Hannah, quite well, as well as the wives of the other gunslingers. Her aunt's store was the only one willing to sell to Hannah when her husband had died and her crooked brother-in-law was trying to force her hand in marriage. Hannah had never forgotten that, and her friends were as loyal as she was.

Betty shivered, thinking about how well Callie had written the story and how romantic it had been when Eli had come to Hannah's rescue. She couldn't wait to read Callie's next book, especially since Mirabelle and Billy had gone through a good deal of danger as well.

A wagon pulled by two bays came down the street, and Betty waited until it passed before she crossed. The hotel stood in front of her now, and Betty hesitantly stepped inside. She wasn't quite sure where to go to find Kent or the restaurant's cook. She'd never been inside the hotel before. Luckily, she recognized Clyde behind the large desk and walked toward him.

"Well, hello," he said. "What have you got there?"

"A partial order for the hotel," she answered shyly. "I thought I'd bring it over, since we weren't busy."

"That was kind of you," Clyde said. "I'll be sure—Ah! Mr. Jackson. You have a delivery."

Betty sucked in a breath and turned, trying to push down her excitement at being rewarded with the very person she'd hoped to see. "Hello," she said.

"It's good to see you," Kent said. "Are these the spices?"

"Yes," Betty told him.

"I appreciate you getting them to me so quickly," Kent told her.

Betty noticed Clyde had stepped away to give them a moment of privacy, and appreciated the man for it. It wasn't like their conversation was anything personal, but it was still nice to just be with him.

Kent added, "You didn't have to go to the trouble."

"Oh, I wanted to," Betty assured him. "It's so nice out, it's a pleasure to escape the store for a few moments. Besides," she said, giving in to the smile that emerged, "Gus came in the store to visit Aunt Glinda."

"In that case, I'm delighted you are here," Kent told her. "Have you ever been inside the hotel before?"

"No." Betty shook her head. "It's much larger than I imagined."

"The hotel stays busy," he told her. "As long as I've owned it, there's never been more than a single room or two empty. If that."

"I hear good things about your restaurant too," Betty told him, as she glanced toward the doors leading to it.

"Join me for lunch one day," Kent told her.

"Oh! I, that is..." Betty was sure her cheeks were red. Had he really just asked her for lunch? That meant she'd be sitting there with him at a small table. Just the two of them. They'd talk and get to know each other and... Shyly, she answered, hoping that he hadn't thought she was trying to finagle an offer, "I'd love to."

He grinned at her, and reached his fingers toward the small box on the counter. Betty placed her hands on it, gently scooting the wooden box closer to him. His skin brushed hers, and Betty sucked in a breath, not caring if her cheeks felt—and likely looked—-as though they were sunburned.

"Will Thursday work?" Kent asked her softly, his eyes locked on hers. "I'd love to get to spend more time with you. I'm glad you said yes."

"Thursday is perfect," Betty told him, amazed she was able to speak without stammering. "We aren't usually too busy then. My aunt can easily manage on her own for a time."

A noise from the street made them both turn, and Betty mourned the loss of the fleeting contact. She clasped them together before her and said, "I'd best go. The rest of your order should be in soon."

"I'll look forward to Thursday," Kent told her. "Noon?"

"Noon," Betty echoed, and left the hotel.

She wanted to look behind her, to see if he was still there, but as she started to turn her head, two men knocked her on either side of her arms. They jostled her backward, and Betty frowned.

"Sorry," one of the men, who had several missing teeth, said. He tipped his hat. "Wasn't looking where I was going."

"That's right," the other said, sneering as he looked her up and down in a way Betty didn't like at all.

"Quite all right," Betty said, and tried to walk around them, but the men pressed closer, and again, bumped her.

"Oops," one said, though there was no humor in his face. His eyes were locked on hers, almost challenging her as if to see how she'd react. Betty wasn't really sure what she should do. Every bit of her felt on high alert, and her instinct was saying to run.

"Excuse me," Betty said, her voice trembling.

"Is there a problem?" Eli asked, having come over from across the street. His eyes were as cold as steel, and his hands rested on the gun belt at his hips. "You gentlemen look to be having a little trouble walking. We've got a jail cell you can sober up in."

Betty looked up from where she'd been staring at the ground, not wanting to see the smirking faces of the men before her. She was relieved to see Eli, and to notice how the men had stepped back. At the same moment, Kent appeared at her shoulder, glaring at the two men who were chuckling and making their way into the hotel.

"Are you hurt?" he asked her, looking her over quickly in a way that Betty didn't mind at all. It was a stark contrast to how she'd felt when the other two had stared at her. With Kent, she felt concern coming from him. The other men had been something else. She wasn't sure what, but it had felt alarming.

"Knocked into her, one on each side," Eli said. Betty didn't miss how he raised an eyebrow, and looked at Kent, adding, "Looked a little like a setup. Kept doing it."

"A setup?" Betty asked, confused. What did that mean? She glanced at Kent, and was surprised to see his face was one of fury. She tried to reassure him. "I'm sure it was just an accident."

"It won't happen again," Kent promised her, his eyes flashing.

"I'll walk you back," Eli told her. "To the store?"

"I can manage," Betty assured him. "Thank you, though." She gave the gunslinger and Kent a small smile and hurried over to her aunt's general store. She knew both men were watching her, and gave a wave before she walked through the doors.

That had been strange. What had Eli meant? Did he mean the two men had walked into her on purpose? And if so, why? And why had Kent looked so angry? Maybe he was feeling protective. That thought sent a shiver through

Betty. She wouldn't mind that at all. The lunch invitation for Thursday filled her thoughts suddenly. She couldn't wait to see him again, and also to thank him for looking after her when the men came up to her. Hopefully, she'd never see either of them again.

"There you are," her aunt said as she walked in. "You've got a letter."

Betty walked over and took the envelope her aunt had placed on the counter. It was from her parents. She didn't want to open it, but did, skimming over the contents. Her mother's small, neat handwriting told her all the news back home, especially that of a wedding date settled on for her sister once her intended returned from a business trip. Her mother had even written out every detail about the menu, dress, and guest list.

Slowly, Betty refolded the letter and placed it back into the envelope.

"All is well?" her aunt asked.

"Yes. Mostly wedding details," Betty answered with a smile she didn't feel. Her soul ached, and it felt as though her heart had broken.

Oh, she didn't fault her sister for falling in love. But did she have to do it with him? With the man she'd been dreaming of from the day she'd first seen him? Sam had been walking past when she and her sister were leaving the store and a child had knocked into them, sending their parcels to the ground. Sam had stopped, helping to retrieve them, his warm smile and rich voice sending shivers through her.

It didn't matter, though. He'd hardly taken his eyes off of her sister. Betty knew she shouldn't have, but in the weeks afterward, when they'd seen him now and again at the park or in the shops, she wished he'd notice her, not her sister.

Even now, the memory pained her. Her lower lip quivered, and she tried to hold back the tears that threatened to fall. It didn't matter. He hadn't chosen her. Hadn't even looked at her. The moment he'd asked to marry her sister, she stopped even thinking there might be a chance with him. He was her sister's now, and she...well, Betty was without even the hope of a romance.

She'd forgotten, though, moved on. So, why was she so upset? Kent seemed interested in her. Were these tears because she was really afraid that, once again, something would happen and she'd lose the man she was interested in? This one being Kent?

Betty put the letter into the pocket of the apron she tied on. "I'll write them later," she said. "If there's anything you'd like me to include, just let me know."

"I'll write your mother a note," her aunt decided, "and slip it in there."

With a nod, Betty found something to do to keep herself busy. She ought not to feel so miserable. After all, today she'd gotten to see Kent. They'd touched, and he'd invited her for lunch. She shouldn't let the joy she'd felt be diminished. But it seemed to her that her sister had uncanny timing. Oh, she knew it wasn't her mother's fault for writing, nor her sister's fault that the letter detailing her sister's happiness arrived today, but it still felt that way.

What made things even more difficult was that no one, not her parents, not her sister, and not even her aunt knew just how much Betty had been suffering. Not a one of them had realized how much she'd foolishly hoped for the attention of the man who didn't choose her.

Betty's eyes drifted to the hotel. She just hoped she wouldn't witness Kent falling for someone before she had a chance to get to know him better and see if there could be something between them. She honestly didn't expect anything to come of their lunch, but a pleasant diversion to ease her suffering a little wouldn't be unwelcome.

It also might be all she could hope for.

Chapter 5

"What were you thinking? You promised you wouldn't cause trouble," Kent snarled, throwing his hands up in the air as he nearly spat the words.

"Couldn't resist," Harry said. "She's a pretty one."

"Always fun to watch how they shy away," Jimbo said. "Though, didn't take too kindly to that man—or you—spoiling my good time."

"That man," Kent hissed, "was Eli Jones. The famed gunslinger."

"*Was* is right," Harry said. "Don't nobody who hangs up their hat stay sharp. We don't got nothing to worry about from him."

It was pointless to argue with them. So, Kent asked, trying to keep his tone even, "Why are you here?"

"We just are, Kenty boy," Harry said. "And when we're done with what we're doing, we'll be gone."

"Are you looking for a mark?" Kent asked. "There's nothing here."

"We need a little something to get us to our next stop," Jimbo admitted. "Running low on loot that ain't hot."

"Hot? Do you mean…" Kent took a deep breath. "Have you got stolen goods with you? Is there a bounty on you?"

"Aw, heck no!" Harry answered. "You know we never go so big as to get a bounty on us. You worry too much. Just need a place to lie low for a little. Soon as things cool off, we're gone."

Kent closed his eyes and put his hands to his temples. "I shouldn't have let you stay," he said. "I'm trying to build a life, and you're ruining it."

"That the gratitude we're getting?" Harry asked. "Saved you as a young pup. Figure you owe me."

"I've paid, and then some," Kent said. He stalked to the hotel suite door. "Lie low, but make it quick. Then get out. And don't you dare get near or touch Betty again."

"Betty, huh?" Harry asked, crossing his arms. "Well, maybe Betty don't want that. Maybe she wants me. You saw her acting all coy."

Kent crossed the room and grabbed Harry's collar before it had registered with him. Just as quickly, he realized this was what Harry wanted, to make him angry.

"You're no fun no more," Jimbo said. "Reckon we're better off without you."

Kent didn't answer, just glared at each of them as he released Harry and left, quietly closing the door behind him. White-hot anger, so intense he could hardly hold it in filled him. He stopped and leaned against the wall for a moment.

He could handle this. He was sure. Just a few days more, then maybe he could get them to go. Meanwhile, he'd better be sure not to draw any more attention to his hotel. Two incidents in two days? Folks were going to talk, and the gunslingers might take matters into their own hands. It wouldn't be good for business.

And Betty. He wanted—no, needed—to apologize to her. He also had to let her know he wasn't going to let anything happen to her. She'd looked so frightened, and Eli... He knew the gunslinger was feeling suspicious of his former partners.

Kent hurried to the front of the hotel. "Clyde, can you watch things for me?" Kent asked. "I need to do something."

"Sure, not a problem," Clyde said. Then he hesitated. "Those friends of yours...think they'll do that again? Betty looked right shook up."

"I hope not," Kent answered grimly. "I talked to them. And I'm heading over now to apologize to her again. I hope it was just an accident. But..." He stopped. How to say it? How to explain that he was a man with a past? That he had given that up, was wanting to start fresh but had to be careful because Harry and Jimbo might not keep it secret otherwise. Could he even say it? Should he?

"You don't need to explain, sir," Clyde said. "My brother is a bit of a black sheep. Got himself in trouble with the wrong sort, and never wanted to find his way out. I don't hold you responsible for the actions of your friends, former or not. Takes a good man and a lot of effort to choose the harder path."

"Thank you," Kent said, meaning every word. "I appreciate it."

Clyde simply nodded, and Kent walked out of the hotel and toward the general store. When he pushed inside, the first woman he laid eyes on was Mrs. Stover. While polite enough, he sensed she mistrusted him. The woman had a good reason for it, but he still didn't like it. If too many people started looking at him that way, then it was possible that he'd be forced to leave town. If for no reason other than that people wouldn't do business at the hotel.

While there would always be those traveling through, a good portion of his income came from the restaurant, as it was open for three meals a day, and the town was large enough there wasn't any competition with Madge's diner.

"I didn't expect to see you so soon," Mrs. Stover said. "Was there a problem with the spice order?"

"No, everything is fine, thank you," Kent said, even though he hadn't checked it. He didn't intend to complain, even if it wasn't right. If something was missing, he'd simply order more. "No, what I wanted was to speak with Betty, if I may?"

"I'll get her," Mrs. Stover said, though he didn't quite miss the brief second the shop owner's lips pressed together. "She's just making us some tea. One moment."

"There's no rush," Kent assured her, and moved toward the display of sweets. Perhaps while he was here, he'd buy some. He'd thought of having a small packet with three or four penny candies at check-in for the guests. If it would get Mrs. Stover to relax, he'd buy all she had today.

Just then, Betty came into the shop through a door Kent guessed must lead to the living quarters. "Oh, hello," she said, slightly breathlessly as she put a tray down on the counter with a teapot and two cups.

"Hello," Kent said, suddenly feeling awkward. He'd wanted to apologize, set things straight. So, why was he now feeling so awkward about the whole situation?

"Earlier," Kent started, and then stopped. "Well, I mean, I just wanted to—"

The shop bell tinkled, and a woman with her teenage daughters came in.

"Mrs. Height," Mrs. Stover said, "how delightful to see you." She hurried out from behind the counter, and Kent found himself happily alone with Betty. Well, as alone as one could be in a small store with several others.

"I think I know what you are trying to say," Betty told him. "I'm quite fine, thank you. It was just...a little unnerving, and made me frightened for a moment."

"I'm sure no harm was intended," Kent said, even as he knew that might not be the truth. He didn't think they wanted to hurt her, but his friends had always enjoyed pushing their weight around and intimidating people.

She didn't answer, and he added, "I...I know them. Years ago, we were friends. We've drifted apart, and it was unexpected when they showed up. But I spoke with them. I won't let anything—or anyone—hurt you," he quickly added, aware that he was stammering and likely starting to look and sound like a fool.

"I appreciate that," Betty said softly, looking down at her hands, which were resting on the tall wooden counter. "Are we still having lunch together on Thursday?"

"I wouldn't miss it for anything," Kent said, feeling relieved that she appeared to be willing still, especially after she knew now those two men were his friends.

"I'm looking forward to it," Betty told him, giving that sweet, shy smile he loved.

"Betty, will you help me a moment?" her aunt called across the shop. "Fetch a notepad and pencil."

"Go ahead," Kent said. "I don't want to keep you. I just wanted to check on you. That's all."

"It was very kind of you to do so," Betty answered as she stepped from behind the counter. "I'll see you soon."

She was over next to her aunt before he could answer, and with another quick look her way, Kent stepped back outside. He closed his eyes for half a second, as Clyde's words about choosing the harder path replayed in his mind.

He thought he'd been doing so well, but seeing his former partners was bringing up things he didn't want to remember, and the fact that, sometimes, he'd enjoyed the things he'd done with them. Many a time he'd felt proud of how he'd outsmarted a mark.

Kent sighed and opened his eyes, and then startled. Someone was waiting for him.

"Eli," Kent said, a little surprised. Had the gunslinger thought of more that he wanted to say to him? Had he decided to run his friends out of town? Kent wouldn't have minded one bit, though he wasn't sure there were grounds for such a thing, as of yet. But it was the "yet" that he was trying—desperately—to avoid.

"Kent," Eli answered by way of greeting. "Let's walk a little."

With a nod, Kent fell into step with him, and they walked along Red Ridge's main street.

"I'm a little concerned about those guests of yours," Eli said.

“Former friends,” Kent said. “Emphasis on the former part. But I’m...I’m not wanting trouble. Not from them, and not for me or my hotel. The hotel is my business. It’s how I make my living. I don’t want to invite difficulties.”

“I understand,” Eli said mildly. “Just like I know you understand we don’t want trouble in the town. The boys and I have worked too hard to get rid of it, so each time it starts to creep in, we’re going to be there, making sure it gets taken care of.”

Kent swallowed hard.

“That’s all I wanted,” Eli told him. Then the gunslinger stopped, and added, “I’ll be bringing Hannah by for dinner one night soon. She’s been hoping for that strawberry pie your chef made last time we were there. You know when that will be on the menu?”

“Fridays,” Kent answered. “Every Friday this month.”

“Much obliged,” Eli said, walking away.

Kent realized they were just past the hotel, and turned around so he could get back to work. He tried to keep the scowl off of his face as he was walking in, but then caught sight of Jimbo walking into the livery and didn’t bother to hide the expression.

Of course he didn’t want trouble. He’d meant every word. Red Ridge was his home now, and he wanted to keep it that way. He just hoped his friends didn’t do anything stupid, because the last thing he wanted was for the gunslingers and any friends they had nearby to chase the three of them out of town.

Kent didn't want to go back to the way things had been. Couldn't go back. He was an honest man now, even if it took a whole lot of convincing sometimes to remind himself of that.

Chapter 6

"I'm not sure you should go," Betty's aunt said, pressing her lips together. "I'm still not decided on that man."

"Aunt Glinda," Betty sighed. "Please don't go acting like Mother. Though in this instance she'd likely send me, and with an entire list of things to say so he'd ask for my hand. This isn't anything romantic. I'm old enough to have lunch in a public place with a friend without it causing a spectacle."

"Just see it stays that way," her aunt said. "In public." She hesitated, and said, "After last night..."

Betty wrapped her arms around herself. "Yes," she agreed, her voice low. Though she didn't think Kent had anything at all to do with the fact their shop door had been forced open last night—and she was sure her aunt felt the same—Betty knew her aunt was still wary of the *newcomer*, as she called him.

Thankfully, neither of them had noticed anything missing, and Gavin had come over and taken a look, but Betty knew that she and her aunt would be a bit more on edge until someone either confessed or was caught.

The shop door opened, and her aunt's face suddenly brightened. "No rush, dear. Have a good time."

Betty blinked, wondering at the sudden change in her aunt's reaction, until she saw who had come into the store and was slowly shuffling his way toward the counter.

"Hello, Gus," she greeted, as she slipped past the old man.

"Watch fer rain," he warned her, and Betty paused. Gus tapped his knee. "It's a coming."

"Thank you for the warning," Betty told him, and peered upward as she walked outside. Though the sky was blue, clouds did appear to be gathering, some of them with hints of gray. Out here, weather changes happened rapidly. Luckily, if it did start to rain, her aunt's shop wasn't too far from the hotel, and she'd be able to stay mostly dry as she dashed to it.

As Betty started to cross the street, she hesitated. Though she was meeting Kent, they hadn't said where. She'd just assumed she was to walk into the hotel. But was that right? Or should she go to the restaurant? Nerves overtook her then. She didn't want to look foolish by doing the wrong thing.

Betty moved closer, her eyes roaming the front of the building. She'd just go inside, she guessed. Walk up to the counter where Clyde would likely be, explain that she was—

"Are you all right?"

Betty gasped, as her hands grabbed onto the solid chest of the person before her. She'd been so lost in thought, she'd walked straight into someone. "I'm so sorry," she said, looking upward. Betty relaxed just a fraction when she realized it was Kent she'd bumped into. Then, she blushed out of embarrassment, and pulled her hands away as though he were a hot stove. "Forgive me, I was distracted and not looking where I was going. Gus had mentioned rain and I..." She stopped, sure she sounded foolish.

"It happens," Kent said, as he smoothly stepped to her side and offered his arm. "And the way the clouds are gathering makes me think he's right. Hungry?"

"Yes, thank you," Betty said, resting her hand lightly on his arm, and following him into the hotel just as rain started to fall.

As before, the hotel's interior nearly overwhelmed her. The hotel looked like such a restful place. She could see herself sitting in the lobby sipping tea, or even perhaps outside, at a small table.

"Have you thought of making the garden bigger?" Betty asked. "Perhaps offering a tea service there in the warmer months?"

"That's a wonderful idea," Kent told her. "I'd wanted to make the garden area larger, and even considered that guests could enjoy tea there, but I hadn't thought about offering tea and other refreshments."

"You might be able to get the ladies' auxiliary to help with the garden," Betty told him. "Several of those ladies, especially Mrs. Blackstone, are gifted in that way."

"I will see if they'd be willing to help me," Kent said, leading her toward a small table for two next to a window that overlooked the few rosebushes the hotel had. Raindrops slid down the glass windowpanes.

A waitress came over to them, and Betty ordered tea and the soup, while Kent ordered coffee and a sandwich. Once they were alone again, he asked, "Do you garden yourself?"

"Oh no," Betty laughed. She held up one of her hands. "Do you see this thumb? It doesn't look it, but it's quite black. Whatever I touch in the garden seems to wither. So, my mother set me to weeding back home. Somehow, those flourished under my ministrations."

Kent joined in her laughter. "I've got one of those myself," he admitted. "Hence my hesitation in expanding until I can find someone to be my gardener. I'm still finding my way about the town."

"Are you enjoying being here?" Betty asked. She liked that this was the first time they'd been able to meet and talk, just the two of them, outside of the general store.

"I am," Kent told her. "I never imagined I'd own a hotel. Once I tired of driving the stagecoach, I always thought I'd do something with horses or cattle. But now that I'm here, this feels right. Like I was meant for it. I don't know how to describe it any other way."

"I think I know what you mean," Betty told him. "I felt that way the moment I stepped into my aunt's store. Though I'd never worked in one before, I just felt...suited. As though I belonged there."

"Is your being here just temporary?" Kent asked.

Betty hoped that was a hint of disappointment she'd noted in the question. She gave a small shrug. "I don't know. I'd like to stay, but I've not talked to my aunt about it. Truthfully, I feel more at home here than...well, at home. So, I'm in no hurry to leave." She frowned. "I hope I'm not made to."

"Why might that happen?" Kent asked.

Betty hesitated. "My parents are the worrying kind," she finally admitted. Their meals arrived, and she waited until the waitress had left again before saying, "Once she hears Aunt Glinda's store was broken into, they might make me go home."

"When did this happen?" Kent asked, concern written on his face.

"Last night or early this morning," Betty told him. "We don't quite know. When we came downstairs, we saw the back door had been forced open."

"Was anything stolen?"

She shook her head. "Not that we could see. We went all over the store, and nothing looked out of place. Aunt Glinda keeps her money in a safe too."

"That's good," Kent said. "Still." He frowned and picked up his sandwich. "I dislike hearing that."

"I just hope it doesn't happen again," Betty said. She didn't want to admit that it had scared her badly.

Kent seemed to realize that, though, and reached for her hand. "Promise me if you need me, you'll come get me or send word. I'll look after you however I can. As a matter of fact, you and your aunt can come stay at the hotel if you want. I've a vacant room you can use. At no charge."

"That's very generous of you," Betty told him, "but it's unnecessary. While I will tell her, Aunt Glinda won't leave the shop, and I won't leave her. Besides, if word got out?" She shrugged. "Why, someone might take advantage to clear out the whole place!"

"I hadn't thought of that," Kent admitted.

"I wouldn't have either," Betty said, "but it was the first thing Aunt Glinda said. She's very clever."

"So are you," Kent said. Then he stammered, "I mean, well." He stopped, and said, "I hope that didn't offend you."

"Why would it?" Betty asked.

"I don't know," he said. "I just don't want you to think I'm trying to be too familiar too quickly."

Her heart sped up. "Too quickly?" she asked. Then, she whispered, "Does that mean that you'd like to get familiar?"

"I would," Kent told her. He hesitated for a moment, and then reached across the table, resting his hand near hers, which she'd placed on the table. "Would you...would you let me?"

Betty nodded. "I'd like that."

"So there's no one else? No one I'd be stepping on?"

Kent stared at her intently. It made her shiver a little, but Betty liked it. No, she loved it.

"No one," she told him. "I've never had a beau."

She wasn't going to tell him that she'd once been interested in someone. Not if Kent was seemingly interested in her. It was foolish, perhaps it was even selfish or slightly dishonest of her, but she didn't want to risk losing his future affections, if they were to grow.

"You've just made me incredibly happy," Kent told her. "If it's all right with you, I'll stop over later, and ask your aunt for permission to call?"

"I'd like that," Betty told him. She wasn't sure what her aunt would say, but she hoped it would be a yes, and nothing more.

The waitress stopped over, with two plates heaped with strawberries and cream and pound cake. As Betty leaned back slightly for hers to be set before her, someone walking along the sidewalk caught her attention.

She frowned, and then brushed at her eyes, as though she wasn't seeing correctly.

"Is everything okay?" Kent asked her. "You're squinting."

"Yes," Betty said, turning her attention back to Kent. "I just thought I saw someone, that's all."

But it couldn't have been. No, he was back in Colorado, preparing to wed her sister. There must have just been someone passing through who looked like Sam.

As Kent told Betty the story of how he'd obtained the hotel, she nodded along, but only half listened. The man had passed by again, and this time there was no mistaking it.

It was Sam. He was here. But...why? Goosebumps went up her arms and the hairs on her neck prickled in a terrible way. Betty didn't know what was happening or why Sam was in Red Ridge, but she had a feeling that nothing good would come of it.

Chapter 7

Kent glanced up from the check-in desk as Harry and Jimbo left the restaurant dining room. He let his eyes slide away, not wanting to invite any conversation. So far, the two had laid low, keeping to themselves in their suite or walking around the town. That suited Kent just fine. He still didn't know when they'd be leaving.

It had been almost a week since they'd arrived. Neither Harry nor Jimbo seemed anxious to get going. Kent wondered what that meant.

That wasn't the only thing he wondered about. Just as often as not, Betty went through his thoughts, with her sweet face and adorable nose and her uninhibited laugh that set her eyes a sparkling. He couldn't get enough of her and longed to see her again soon. It had been four days since their lunch together. Four long days since he'd had the chance to stare into her eyes, brush his hand against hers, and—

"Watch it," Harry growled.

Kent snapped his attention toward the commotion going on outside. He moved so quickly, his neck hurt. His legs were moving before he realized it, but then he stopped. Harry was in the street, and not directly in front of the hotel. It wasn't his place to intervene.

Yet.

Harry shoved a man and kept going, Jimbo next to him. Kent gritted his teeth. He had to get rid of them, the sooner the better.

"Nice guests you've got," the sheriff said as he strode in.

Kent didn't know how to answer. Most anything he said could incriminate him. He didn't want that. He wanted to stay in Red Ridge. Run his hotel. See Betty.

"Relax. They aren't why I'm here. This time," Gavin said.

"Then how can I help you?" Kent asked. He didn't relax though. Despite what the sheriff said, he wasn't feeling optimistic about the conversation's future subject.

"Have you had any trouble? Beyond those two gents?" Gavin asked, though Kent couldn't tell what he was getting at. The sheriff's face was neutral, and in a man like that, it might not have been a good thing.

Even before he'd come to this town, Kent had heard stories about Gavin Jefferson. So, it was quite a surprise to discover the man had set up home here. Still, he was bound to answer, and so far, the sheriff had been nothing but congenial to him.

"Trouble? What kind?" Kent asked as his brows furrowed. He thought as hard as he could, but nothing stood out. Not at the hotel, not at the restaurant. Unless something had happened, and Clyde hadn't mentioned it yet. The man was still out enjoying his lunch break.

"There have been a few break-ins," the former gunslinger explained, moving his hands to his waist. "The blacksmith had a few small tools stolen. Same with the shoemaker."

"No, nothing like that has happened here," Kent replied. "No break-ins at the hotel, but Betty Doyle—Mrs. Stover's niece—was speaking to me a few days ago. She said someone forced in their shop door. There hasn't been more trouble there, has there? I've not seen her since."

"No, nothing more there. Hopefully, there's nothing else at all. I've got a few extra men, ones fast on the draw, situated around town. We'll keep the place safe."

"I don't doubt it," Kent said. "But why are you telling me?"

"So you can pass it along to your friends," Gavin answered, his voice steely. Before Kent could answer, the sheriff raised a hand. "I know there's a little more to their story and yours than you've let on. You want to talk, you know where my office is. Meantime, feel free to pass along that warning. This is our town, and we'll be shooting first and asking questions later."

"Understood," Kent said.

And he did. The warning was clear as the spring the town got their drinking water from. He just wished his former associates would understand that too. He'd already tried to warn them when they first came, and doubted his mentioning it again would do anything, but Kent planned to do it anyway.

Gavin nodded and left the hotel. Kent hesitated, then walked to the front of the hotel and peered into the street. What were Harry and Jimbo up to? He hoped nothing. Though, doing nothing for those two could be dangerous.

His curiosity was rewarded a moment later, when he watched as Harry and Jimbo left Mrs. Stover's shop. Kent tensed every muscle. Why had they been in there? Were they bothering Betty?

Without even pausing to think, Kent nearly bolted over to them. "I told you to leave her alone," he hissed to Harry. "What were you doing in there?"

"Why, just a bit of shopping, Kenty boy," Harry said in a jovial tone. "Got me a new hat."

Jimbo flicked his wrist, and a small but sharp-looking knife gleamed in the sun. "Got me a new blade."

"The sheriff stopped by," he said, ignoring their purchases. "Had a warning."

"Fool man, always getting in the way," Harry grumbled. "Never seen one so up in a town's business. How much will it take to get him off our backs?"

"He can't be bought," Kent answered.

"Sure, he can," Harry argued. "Every man has his price." Harry started toward the hotel and smacked Kent's shoulder. "Even you have one."

"No, I don't," Kent said, jaw clenched. "I told you. I've gone straight."

"You say," Harry said, pausing. He turned to face Kent, and continued, "But like I said, every man has a price. The thing that keeps him under control. Yours is that woman."

Kent tried not to still, to let it show he was rattled. Instead, he answered, "The sheriff's honest. I wouldn't try to test him."

"He was a gunslinger," Jimbo said with a shrug. "Ain't always honest men."

"This one is," Kent said. "I—"

"Mr. Jackson? I'm sorry to interrupt. The handyman needs to speak with you before he can get started on Room Six."

Kent looked over to where Clyde had appeared next to his elbow and forced a polite look on his face. "Excuse me," he told Harry and Jimbo. "Won't be but a moment."

Kent followed Clyde, and listened as the handyman asked a few questions pertaining to the painting Kent wanted done. By the time he finished, Kent was anxious to get back to his friends, and use Gavin's warning as an excuse to get them to leave town.

However, when he looked around the hotel lobby, they were gone. Now what should he do? Kent thought it over carefully. The idea of letting Harry and Jimbo be caught and, hopefully, swept out of his life forever was appealing.

But Harry, though he wasn't right about many things, was right on this one. Every man had a price. And his *was* Betty. He wouldn't put it past the man to have set something in place to ensure his cooperation or quiet. Which meant that Kent was going to have to figure this out, and fast.

Chapter 8

Betty felt impatient. Her aunt had joined Gus for a bite in the diner. Ordinarily, she wouldn't have minded such a thing, but Aunt Glinda had been leaving the store quite a bit over the last few days, which meant Betty was in charge entirely.

And, again, she wouldn't usually mind, except for the fact it had meant she had to stay in the store. Kent hadn't been able to come in; he'd also had no reason to, and when she did get to leave the store in the evenings and went for a walk, the hotel's dining room was so busy, she was sure that Kent was swamped. That also might be part of why she'd not seen him since the day after their lunch.

True to his word, he'd asked her aunt for permission to call on her. Betty had sensed the hesitation in her aunt's voice, but she'd agreed. Someone from the hotel had come after Kent before he and Betty had the chance to make future plans. She couldn't help it. She was worried that maybe he'd changed his mind about spending time with her. Was that why he'd not stopped in?

Feeling impatient with her aunt, Betty wandered to the window, hoping to see her returning. Then, she'd ask permission to leave for a short time herself. But though Betty looked up one side of the street and the other, she couldn't see her.

Irritation filling her, Betty walked to the counter, reaching it just as the door's bell tinkled. "Hello," she called as she turned.

Betty wished she hadn't. Wished her aunt were there. Wished anyone, even her least favorite customers were there. A terrible wrongness filled the store, creeping and crawling, winding its way and filling the air with a heaviness that made her stomach feel sick.

"Well, hello there, girlie," one of the men who'd deliberately knocked into her said, moving closer.

It was all Betty could do not to shudder. Instead, she pulled herself as tall as she could, and asked, her voice perhaps a little tight, "What can I help you gentlemen find?"

"Gentlemen!" the man hooted. "You hear that, Jimbo?"

"Sure do, Harry," the second man said, letting his eyes roam over her. "Heard it and liked it."

The shudder escaped, and Betty just hoped the whimper of fear hadn't. "Did you want to just browse?" she asked, hoping that neither of the men would fill their pockets with her aunt's merchandise. However, if they did, then the sheriff could arrest them. The thought didn't upset her in the least. And, if they were busy, she could get help. Perhaps that's what she should do anyway. Find someone else to come in.

Betty casually picked up the broom that was behind the counter. "I was just about to sweep the front," she said as she started toward the door.

"Naw, you ain't," Harry said. "I want to be waited on. Like the gentleman you said I is."

"Of course," Betty said, her voice brittle. "What are you looking for today?"

"Purdy girl," Jimbo answered, moving far too close for her liking. "One 'bout your height, your coloring, smells like you." He licked his lips. "Matter of fact, I'll just take you."

"Now, now," Harry said, though she saw his eyes never left her, as she flicked her own between the two men, "Kenty boy says we can't touch her."

"Didn't say nothing about looking," Jimbo said. "So I'm gonna look real good."

The door opened just then, and Betty all but collapsed in relief as her aunt and Gus walked in. There was disappointment on Harry's and Jimbo's faces, but both men stopped talking to her. Harry picked up a hat, and Jimbo examined a knife, taking their time about it.

Betty tried not to tremble. She didn't want to upset her aunt or put dear old Gus in any danger. She knew he'd try and protect her and her aunt, but might be overwhelmed by two men half his age and much larger.

"We'll take these," Harry said, reaching in his pocket for some money.

Betty nodded. "That will be four dollars and fifty cents," she said. "Would you like them wrapped?"

"No," Harry said, leaning in so close it was almost a whisper.

She jerked backward, not sure why he'd done that. Harry laughed, plopping the hat on his head and moving toward the door, Jimbo right behind him.

Another customer came in, and Betty saw it was Hannah, who was frowning as the two men left.

"I don't think I like them," Hannah said. "Who are they?"

"Guests at the hotel," Betty said. "And I don't like them either."

She wanted to tell her friend what had happened, both the first time she'd met them and now, but for her aunt's sake, she didn't.

"No matter," Betty continued. "Are you here for some shopping?"

"Yes," Hannah said, handing over a list. "Gus, if you're all done in town, I have the wagon."

"Reckon I might ride back with you then," Gus agreed. "Help you carry yer goods."

Betty worked on filling the list, and then waved goodbye as Hannah and Gus left. She sighed, and leaned against the counter. Her aunt was back, but now she didn't want to go to the hotel. She was too scared she'd run into the two men again.

"Betty, have you written to your parents yet?"

Betty startled, then shook her head. "Not yet, Aunt Glinda. "I...I wasn't sure what to say. I wanted to wait just a little longer before telling them about Kent."

Another customer came in, and Betty busied herself straightening the stock while her aunt helped the customer. She knew she needed to write to her mother, but what was she to say? She didn't want her parents to think she was mentioning Kent to take the focus off her sister's wedding.

She also didn't want her sister thinking that because her parents might be overjoyed that Betty might have a chance at a beau.

The word made her mind flash back to the man she'd seen through the window. It wasn't her sister's intended; that would be impossible. And it was something she wouldn't mention in the letter. So, what could she write?

About how wonderful all of the wedding plans sounded? How she hoped her sister would be happy?

The words felt hollow, and even though Betty no longer felt the ache she once had when her sister had announced her engagement, the fact remained there was such an awkward feel about the entire situation. An uncomfortableness that Betty didn't care for.

Just then, a man walking past the store caught Betty's attention. She frowned and took a few steps closer. It was the same man she'd seen when she was having lunch with Kent. And there was no mistaking it now. That wasn't a stranger, and it wasn't a coincidence. That was Sam. The man her sister was to marry. In all of the happenings, she'd forgotten all about him. Now, her worry flooded back.

Why was he here? And, should she tell her aunt? Betty wasn't sure. What could have brought Sam to Oregon, from Colorado? She recalled her mother's letter mentioning business, but what kind of business would he have that would have taken him so far?

Betty wasn't quite sure what Sam did for a living, and wasn't sure her sister had ever said, but it didn't seem right that he'd be here, in Red Ridge.

Unless...

She shook her head. No, that couldn't be it. Sam wouldn't have come all this way for her. To tell her he'd chosen the wrong sister. Would he?

For just a moment, Betty let that idea play through her mind, creating a scenario where he begged for forgiveness, and then pleaded for her hand. But, though a few weeks ago the idea would have delighted her, now Betty felt nothing. She wasn't interested in Sam. Had she ever been? When she thought about it, it had never felt like it had with Kent.

She'd moved on. Her heart had moved on. Yet, seeing him... Betty drew in a deep breath. She hoped it was just her imagination, but things were happening in town that made her nervous. The strangers who seemed interested in her, the break-ins, and now Sam. Was any of it connected?

But as soon as she thought that, she quickly dismissed the idea. Why would it be? Still, something wasn't right. The feel of eyes watching her told her so. Betty sucked in another breath and tried to calm the racing of her heart. She knew Kent had meant it, that he'd help her if needed. But what if her aunt was right? What if Kent couldn't be trusted?

Had she let herself fall for a criminal?

Chapter 9

Stars lit the skies, and the moon seemed overly large. Kent liked it when it looked that way. He wasn't a scientific man, so didn't know why it happened, and only sometimes, just like he didn't know why many nights the moon was white, and others a golden color, but it still made him wonder.

It had been hard to sleep. Thinking about things—such as the moon—kept his mind busy from the two other subjects that occupied the rest of his mind. Betty, and his unwelcome hotel guests.

Kent hoped that by not visiting her, he was protecting her in some way. The hotel had been unusually busy, and every room was full, so it wasn't an excuse if he were to say work had kept him away. But he longed to see her. Assure himself she was well, hold her hand, see her beautiful smile.

However, each time he was tempted to walk to the store, to steal away for a moment and seek her out, he caught sight of Harry or Jimbo, and any hope he had of slipping away vanished as they approached him. It was as though the two had some sort of sixth sense about seeking him out at the time he least wanted them.

Betty's protection was important to him, and Kent refused to take any chances or risk something happening to her. Avoiding her, for now, was the only way he knew how to keep her safe. He wouldn't lie, too, he hoped she'd never find out how well he knew Harry and Jimbo.

It was well after midnight. Kent rubbed at his eyes. He wished he could sleep. Suddenly, every fiber of him tensed as a creak, one he'd deliberately left unfixed outside his door, sounded. Someone was moving in the hallway outside of the suite he lived in.

Quickly moving, ready to defend himself if needed, Kyle opened the door a crack. He was relieved—and then concerned—to see the night manager, a man older than Gus, looking at him mournfully. "Is something wrong?" Kent asked, already starting to pull clothing overtop of his striped pajamas.

"Sorry ter wake ye, Mr. Jefferson. There's just a complaint 'bout noise." The night manager wrung his hands. "I tried knocking at the door where the people said it was coming from, but there weren't no answer."

"Not a problem, Paul. That's what I'm here for," Kent said. "Allow me a moment to finish dressing, and I'll put a stop to it."

Kent hurriedly buttoned his shirt, tucking it into the waistband of his pants, and then headed toward the suite Paul told him the complaint had been made about. With a deep sigh, he raised his hand to knock. Of course. He should have known that it would be this suite. The real surprise was that up until now, there hadn't been any other problems.

Since their arrival, Harry and Jimbo had been quiet. So, what had they been doing that caused so much noise someone would complain? And at this time of night too! For two criminals not wanting to draw attention to themselves, they weren't doing a very good job of it.

Knocking quietly as not to disturb anyone else, Kent waited at their door. No one answered, just like the night manager had said happened to him. He knocked again, and waited. Still no one. Kent was about to go get the key for the room when he decided to just try the knob.

To his surprise, it twisted easily under his hand, and he stuck his head inside the suite. "Hello?" he called out softly. "Harry? Jimbo?"

There was a constant scraping noise from the bedroom. Metal against metal? Kent couldn't place the sound, and started to walk to the door. *I'll just knock*, he thought, *and then hopefully they'll knock it off. Whatever it is.*

As he crossed the sitting room of the suite, Kent noticed the large rug had been pulled back. He moved toward it, intending to flip it back so no one tripped, when he froze.

It wasn't just that the rug had been turned back a goodly portion. One of the floorboards had been cut and pried up. Fury filled him. He knew they'd hidden something they had stolen, but it was so much they felt they had to damage his hotel to hide it? They couldn't just keep it on their person or inside of a bag? A feeling of incredible betrayal ran through him. But what had he expected?

On the one hand, he hoped that if they were digging it up tonight, that it meant they'd be on their way out of town tomorrow. But as Kent walked close to the cache in his hotel floor, his jaw dropped, and with it fell out any hope he'd held.

"What the..." Kent bent over the small cotton sack hidden in the floorboards. It could easily fit in the palm of his hand. It didn't look special, but it must have been, if it was this hidden. "All this for just a tiny pouch?" he wondered aloud.

Kent reached for the pouch, and opened it slowly, loosening the tie around it until the string fell away. He peered inside and closed his eyes briefly before tipping the contents into his palm.

Diamonds fell into his hand, sparkling in the lantern light of the room. Kent studied them for a moment, then dropped them back into the pouch, and returned it to the floorboard.

It was only then he realized how quiet it was. The noise from the other room had stopped. Kent stood, preparing to knock on the other door, in part to let them know he was there but also to ask them to stay quiet the rest of the night, but when he turned, he was met with angry faces.

And a gun pointed at him.

Chapter 10

"Whatcha doing here, Kenty boy?" Harry asked.

Kent knew that tone. It was the one Harry used a moment or two before he shot someone. It was too calm and too reasonable. And Kent hoped he'd be able to fast talk a little to keep himself alive. Hopefully he wasn't out of practice.

"Trying to keep you two out of trouble," he said, nodding toward the hole in the hotel's floor. "There was a complaint and the night manager said he knocked, but had no answer, so he got me. You know how lucky it is I'm here to turn back the carpet and hide what you left out?"

Kent also realized how fortunate it was that Paul hadn't come in. The man might have met an untimely demise. Just then, he caught movement in the bedroom, and a man he hadn't seen before emerged.

"Who's this?" Kent asked.

"New partner," Jimbo said. "On a trial basis that is."

"Sam Douglas," Harry added in. "Not as sharp as you or as nimble with his fingers, but he'll do. Picked him up to crack safes for us."

Still unsure if his former friends were going to shoot him or not, Kent answered in what he hoped was a friendly tone. "Welcome, Sam." He turned back to Harry and sighed. "I can't help you do what you need to do if you're in here making noise that brings others onto you. If I hadn't answered the knock, the night manager would have sent for the sheriff. Then what? You, just leaving your loot here for anyone to find."

He motioned to the rug and shook his head. "Come on, Harry. Not like you to be sloppy."

His former associate frowned. "Rug was up?" He turned to Jimbo and Sam. "Which one of you stupids did that? We put it back, every time. Never know who's coming in. We are lucky it was Kent. Someone on our side." Harry let out a growl of frustration. "You sure the night manager didn't see nothing?"

"I'm sure," Kent said, relieved that the gun had been lowered, and Harry felt reassured he was a friend, not an enemy. "He didn't open the door, only knocked. But this isn't lying low."

"You know," Harry said slowly, "reckon I'd take your advice more, if you weren't so friendly with the law in these here parts."

"I'm just trying to help you," Kent said. "I don't want trouble. You don't want trouble. That's all this is. And I sure can't help it if the sheriff is hanging around. Of course I'm being nice. Keeps us all safe."

"You say so," Sam said suddenly, "but I'm thinking really, you aren't on our side."

"I'm not on anyone's side but my own," Kent said, letting a little of his frustration leak out. "Way it's always been. I've known Harry and Jimbo far longer than you, I'm betting, and they know what I say is the truth. I might have been a thief, but I was always honest."

"It's true," Jimbo said. "That's why we liked you. Could count on you to split the loot fair like."

Silence filled the room, then Harry said, "Fine. I've heard your advice, now here's mine."

Kent turned his attention to him. Harry had a dangerous streak in him, but surely he wouldn't risk his shelter and his cover, would he?

"You're going to keep quiet," Harry said. "About everything you've seen here, everything you know. If you don't, there's going to be a heap of trouble. First, we'll tell everyone how you used to be part of the gang. Had one of the biggest roles."

Kent swallowed, but before he could assure Harry of his silence, the man held up a hand and kept talking. "Next, we'll shoot up the town. Do a little more than the break-ins we've done so far."

"I thought that might have been you," Kent said, his mind flashing back to Betty's unease, when she'd told him about the store being broken into.

"You don't know the half, boy. We've had a busy night," Jimbo chuckled. "The bank, the diner, the little general store you don't stop staring at."

Kent clenched his fists. "I told you—"

"Hesh up. I'm the one talking. After we go around doing that," Harry said, taking a few steps closer, "we'll help ourselves to Betty."

"She's not as pretty as her sister," Sam said, "but she'll do."

Kent's brows furrowed. Not as pretty as her sister? What did that mean? He didn't think Betty's sister was in town, and she'd never shown him a picture, so how would Sam know? He wanted to ask, but if he let on he was curious and worried, that might put Betty in even more danger.

Concern filled him. He knew he hadn't called on her yet, and wondered if she'd been feeling as though he'd changed his mind. Maybe he could get her a note somehow. Both to reassure her of his intentions and to warn her about this Sam fellow.

"...cooks pretty good. Maybe when we're done here, take her along," Sam was saying. "I don't plan to go back to Colorado, but Betty, bet if I ask, she'll join us. She's always been real sweet on me."

Kent's blood ran cold. He did know her. But how? Betty had always seemed so sweet and quiet. But he knew she'd come here from Colorado. Had she been lying to him about why she came? And that there was no one she was involved with?

No, it was a foolish thought. Betty wasn't working with them. Was she? But how else would Sam know her, the way he claimed?

Kent felt dizzy and sick to his stomach. He staggered a few steps to the doorway of the room. The gang hooted in laughter as he stumbled into the hallway.

He leaned against the wall, his head back and a complex feeling of anger and fear, of worry and doubt filling him. Was this part of Harry's plan? Was Sam making things up? Had they learned just enough about Betty to plant these seeds of doubt in his mind?

Why did he ever think he could put the past behind him? It was impossible. And now, he'd brought trouble to the town that was nothing more than welcoming to him and his hotel. There went any chance of building a future, or expanding and making a comfortable life for himself.

Because of Harry and Jimbo, and now this Sam, he'd also ruined any chance of having something with Betty.

That is, if she'd even be interested in him. The way Sam talked, her heart belonged to him. Was she playing two men? And one a criminal? Was she part of this? A criminal herself?

Endless questions swirled in his head, and Kent didn't know what to do. He had to do something, though. He might have gotten to the point where it was too much for him to handle on his own.

Chapter 11

The sudden sound of shattering glass sent Betty bolting from her bed. Somehow, she grabbed her dressing gown that was at the foot of her bed, and wrapped it around her shoulders while flinging open her bedroom door.

Her aunt was already there, a worried look on her face, but a rifle at her shoulder. The sight of it shouldn't have surprised Betty. After all, Aunt Glinda had been living as a woman alone for most of her life, and needed to defend herself, and her son Bill when he was just a baby, but seeing the weapon, and the determination on her aunt's face made her heart feel as though it were about to burst from her chest from the seriousness of the situation.

"Aunt Glinda," Betty whispered. "Do you think we should go downstairs?"

Her aunt pressed her lips together in a moment's thought, then opened the door leading to the steps where the shop was below. They crept down the stairs, her aunt in the lead. On the final step, Betty slid open the shutter on the lantern she held, illuminating the shop.

She blinked a few times, but once her eyes had adjusted—the large moon outside helping—she looked around. There wasn't anyone.

The glass on their door, however, was broken. Betty started toward it, then gasped in alarm as a figure drew close.

"It's me! Billy Madison!" the gunslinger called, and Betty relaxed at once. She could see it was him now.

"Did you see who broke my glass window?" Aunt Glinda asked.

"Didn't," Billy said grimly. "Heard it and came a running. But don't you worry none, Mrs. Stover. I'll sit here the rest of the night and protect the place, and you ladies."

"I don't know if I'll be able to get back to sleep," her aunt said, "but I do appreciate it. Shouldn't you be home with Mirabelle though? Isn't she expecting?"

Even in the dim light, Betty could see the pleased grin come across Billy's face. "She sure is. But she's not alone. Since Gavin and Eli are here in town, Aiden and Ryan too, the girls are all staying together in a couple houses. Nothing's getting through them."

"Good," Aunt Glinda replied. "Then I will worry less." She shook her head. "But I'm right angry about my glass window."

"I'll be sure it gets fixed right away," Billy promised.

"Thank you," Betty said. "We sure appreciate you." Her eyes drifted toward the hotel. "Is there more trouble in town tonight? Other than here?"

"Not yet," Billy said. "It better stay that way. At the sign of anything else, it will be dealt with. Quickly and finally."

He pulled over a chair from the porch where Aunt Glinda kept a checker set, and sat right in front of the door. Though he looked as though he were resting, Betty knew he wouldn't be. His fingers sat lightly on his gun, and Billy was quick on the draw. That, and the fact he was blocking the door, made her feel better. She just wished this hadn't happened.

Betty followed her aunt back upstairs. They each went to their rooms, and Betty was sure her aunt was trying to rest, like she was. However, once she climbed into bed, Betty started shaking.

First the door forced open, and then the shop window broken. Why? Nothing had been taken. Was this simply a tactic to scare them? And who would do such a thing? Betty thought back through everyone in town. She couldn't think of a single person who disliked her aunt.

Maybe it was the two men from the hotel. Harry and Jimbo. But as soon as she thought it, Betty felt bad.

She didn't have any evidence, and it sure wasn't right or Christian-like to accuse someone of doing such things without knowing they had.

Betty tossed and turned, unable to get comfortable. She got up several times and looked through her window to the street below. She couldn't see Billy, but she was sure the gunslinger would keep his word, and protect them and their store all night.

She decided to try and rest, and then think up a proper thank you for him in the morning. Surely, he'd be exhausted, after a sleepless night.

Betty resigned herself to the fact the only way morning would come faster was if she fell asleep, and settled herself in bed once more, closing her eyes. Eventually, sleep did come, and Betty hurriedly dressed. The living area of her aunt's home was vacant, so Betty went downstairs.

She could just see Billy Madison walking away, and his chair was now occupied by Gus.

Her aunt turned to her, concern on her face. "Gus was just telling me what's happened. The bank was broken into. So was the diner. Gavin and Eli have been sitting at the bank overnight, and Ryan and Aiden the diner. Billy and a few other men are joining them to see what the damages were there, now that it's daylight."

"Who would do such a thing?" Betty whispered, bringing her hands to her mouth.

"Don't know," Gus said, "but they're a lowlife. Found Madge's safe. She's hopping mad. Luckily, she'd emptied out most of it, but they still got a few dollars."

"That poor woman," Aunt Glinda sighed.

"Reckon they went there on account of it being so close to the bank. No way they'd get into the bank safe," Gus continued. "Figure, based on the time, your place was hit first."

"It doesn't make sense," Betty said. "None of it. Why would someone break our window but not come inside and take anything?"

"Don't know," Gus answered. "But glad you ladies weren't hurt. Glinda, it might be a day or two before we can get it fixed. I'll be right fine sleeping on the shop floor, or even in this here chair to protect you. Won't let no one get through me. You got my word on that."

"Oh goodness," Betty's aunt said, her cheeks turning pink. "That's not necessary, but you are most kind."

"I mean every word," Gus said.

Betty fought the smile twitching on her lips and went to the back of the store, to give her aunt and Gus as much privacy as possible.

Just then, two men walking in the street caught her eye. It was Harry and Jimbo. A sudden anger filled her. No, she didn't know for a fact they were to blame about her aunt's shop, or the other things that had happened last night, but the smirks on their faces irritated her so much, Betty found herself muttering, "I'll be back shortly," to her aunt and Gus as she walked past, briskly headed toward the hotel.

She was going to ask Kent if he knew something, and why he allowed such men to stay there in his hotel.

And, if she was brave enough, she'd also ask why he hadn't called on her.

Chapter 12

"Wait one moment, Miss. I'll go find him," the front desk manager said.

Betty nodded, and tried not to feel impatient. She went to one of the plush chairs nearby and sat, hoping she looked at ease, and not at all upset and anxious, the way she was feeling.

Though she'd heard the stories of how dangerous Red Ridge had been under the corrupt sheriff, she'd never witnessed it herself. Betty had overheard her aunt and Gus mentioning how it was starting to feel like those days, and couldn't imagine just how terrible they had been. Thank goodness the gunslingers had come along, cleaned up the town, and put it under their protection.

But what was going on now? She got the feeling, just in her short interaction with Billy, something serious was about to happen to someone if such things kept happening.

The sound of footsteps coming closer made Betty look up. "Kent," she said, standing quickly. She smiled, momentarily forgetting everything but how happy she was to see him. Then she saw the strained expression on his face, and the exhaustion. "Are you all right?" she asked.

"I don't know," he admitted, his voice low. "Are you?"

She bit her lip. "Can we talk for a moment?"

"Yes, but not here," Kent told her, glancing around. "Somewhere where no one can overhear us."

"I agree," Betty said. "But where?"

"Let's go for a walk," Kent said, offering his arm. "Then, even if someone hears something, it's only a few words."

That sounded like a good idea. Betty rested her hand on his arm, closing her eyes briefly as tingles went through her fingertips and shot up her arm. This wasn't the time for that. No, this was serious. She needed to focus.

They left the cool shade of the hotel interior and stepped into the bright sunshine. Betty wasn't sure how to start the conversation. Luckily, Kent did.

"I'm glad you stopped by," he said, his voice low. "I've missed you. Things have prevented me from stopping by the general store to call on you."

"I understand," Betty answered, though she didn't. Not really. Then, she looked at him. "Last night, someone broke the glass window of the door to our shop."

"Were you hurt?" Kent asked. "Is your aunt safe? What happened?"

"We are fine," Betty assured him. "Thankfully, there were men watching the town. I hadn't realized that, but evidently they've been suspecting something might happen. Billy Madison came over and sat up all night protecting the shop, and us."

"I'm beholden to him," Kent said, stopping briefly as he looked upward.

"However, that's not all," Betty said.

"What else?" Kent asked.

She hesitated. "Last night, Madge's diner was broken into. They stole the money from her safe. Luckily, she didn't have much there at all. They also broke into the bank. We found out this morning, Aunt Glinda and I. Kent, I...I have to tell you something. I haven't told anyone else, but I have suspicions about who might be behind it."

Was she mistaken in thinking his arm tensed? That the tiny muscles in his cheek clenched, before a curious expression overtook him? Betty wasn't sure.

"Who?" he asked.

"It's none of my business," Betty admitted. "But are your friends trustworthy? Harry and Jimbo?"

"I wouldn't call them friends. But I did know them for a time."

"They...they came in the shop," Betty said quietly. "It scared me how they were acting. It felt as though they knew you quite well. Harry called you Kenty boy."

There was no mistaking it now. Kent's jaw was clenched, and his shoulder taut. "I...I..." He stopped and sighed. "You asked are they trustworthy. No, not at all. I'm extremely concerned about everything going on right now with them, but my biggest concern is keeping you and the town safe."

Kent walked them toward the shade of a large tree, and they stood under its canopy of bright green leaves. The shade was welcome, and allowed her to return his searching expression without the sun causing her to squint.

"What do you mean?" Betty asked in a near whisper. "I feel like something's going on, and you are part of it. Only...only I have this strange sense of you being stuck in the middle. Not one way or the other."

Kent jammed a hand through his thick hair, and groaned, then looked away in the distance. "I'm not sure right now. I'm so confused. I'm also tired. I was awake the entire night. Things happened that I can't talk about right now."

Betty was sure her face had darkened. "Did it have anything to do with the window at our shop getting broken or the bank or the diner?"

"I promise, I'll answer when I can," Kent told her. "But can I ask you something first? You're right. I feel like I'm in the middle. Right now, I'm not sure who I can trust."

Betty felt confusion wash over her, and her brows knitted together. "Of course. You can trust me." Why wouldn't he, she wondered.

"Do you know a fellow named Sam Douglas?" he asked.

All Betty could do was blink. How had he known about Sam?

"I can tell by your expression you do," Kent said. He looked down at her boots. "Will you tell me how? If it's true? You're his?"

"Me? His? What!" Betty sputtered. "No! Sam is supposed to marry my sister." A stabbing pain shot through her, and she pressed her hands to her chest. "I admit, I met him when she did. But as soon as he laid eyes on my sister, I knew there was no one else for him."

"That's not how he was talking," Kent growled.

Betty looked into his face, and tentatively put her hand on his arm. "It's just like how the moment I met you, I knew there was no one else I'd like to get to know better."

"Do you mean that?" Kent asked. "Last night, he was talking and...and I got so confused. It sounded like you two were..."

"I hardly know him," Betty said. Then she took a deep breath. "So, that *was* him I saw through the window. I'd tried to tell myself I was wrong. But how did you start talking with Sam? Is he staying there at the hotel?"

"In a way," Kent answered, taking her hand in his. "He and Harry and Jimbo are..."

"Up to no good?" Betty finished.

"Yes." Kent squeezed her hands gently. "Promise me you'll be careful. I'm trying to fix this. I have a plan. But I'm worried about you and your safety."

"Don't," Betty said. "I can look after myself. That is, until the time comes that you might want to look after me?"

"That time is already here," Kent said, taking her other hand in his, and bringing both to his lips to press a kiss onto her knuckles. "Betty, I'm crazy over you. I want to get to know you better and see if it goes somewhere. But I've got to take care of this first. I'm not ignoring you. I promise. I've just got to keep my distance for a little."

"I understand," Betty said, and this time she did. "Promise me, though, you'll look after yourself. What happiness will I ever have in life, if you aren't here to be with me?"

"Betty," he whispered, and brought a hand to her cheek.

She stepped closer, and into his arms, not caring if it was the least bit wanton. Betty could sense danger filling the town, and if Kent was determined to try and put a stop to it, what if this was the last moment she had to tell him how she felt?

A gentle breeze blew, and as Kent parted his lips to say something, Betty boldly took her chance, doing something that, up until now, she wasn't sure she'd ever have the opportunity to do.

She rose on the tips of her toes, her hands holding on to Kent's warm chest for balance, and brought her lips to his. Everything around them seemed to stop, and Betty knew that she'd never love another man for as long as she lived.

She was also acutely aware that this might be the only time she got to have a moment such as this, especially if Kent was somehow connected to Harry, Jimbo, and Sam. Billy had been warning her and the town when he'd said at the sign of anything else, it would be dealt with. Quickly and finally.

Chapter 13

He had kissed Betty. Actually, Betty had kissed him. Or, maybe they'd done it at the same time? He wasn't sure. All Kent knew was that life would never be the same again.

Without a doubt, he felt much better knowing that Betty wasn't interested in Sam. However, Sam knowing her and his family complicated things. Kent also was feeling guilty for letting himself not trust Betty for a time, but with all that had been going on...

A couple left the restaurant, and Kent raised a hand in farewell. Thankfully, business hadn't slowed, even with all that had been going on. That was one positive thing, at least.

His eyes narrowed in thought. How to get rid of Harry, Jimbo, and now Sam? He had the feeling they were lingering—and had broken into the diner's safe—because they were low on cash. Get them a good-sized payday, and they'd leave right quick, both with the loot and his secret. So, how to make that happen?

He wanted them to leave more than anything. He wanted things to go back to the direction they had been heading in with Betty. And with his business.

Most of all, he wanted them gone. Kent knew how Harry and Jimbo were. They didn't care who got in their way if they wanted something. For the safety of everyone in town, he needed to do something. Even if it might cost him every cent he had. It would be worth it, though.

His attention turned to the front of the building. A man was strolling toward the hotel. Looked like a traveling businessman. His walking stick gleamed, and he twirled it now and again. Kent pulled his eyes away from the mesmerizing sight to take in the sharp suit, dust-free boots and rounded hat. Someone sure didn't frequent dusty places such as Red Ridge. Back in the old days, the man would have been a mark. Now, he was a valued guest. Something he had to remind himself, even as he wondered if the man might have something valuable he could take, as part of the payment to offer Harry, Jimbo, and Sam to leave.

"Welcome, sir," he greeted as the man wandered inside, glancing about as though he owned the place.

Then, Kent's eyes widened as the gentleman stopped before him. "Eli? I didn't recognize you."

It was true. He couldn't ever recall seeing the gunslinger in anything but worn pants and a work shirt, often with his leather duster, and always with his gunbelt. Unless it was a special occasion, that was. Kent glanced at Eli's middle, looking for the weapon. He saw a lump under the jacket, and assumed it was there.

"That's the whole point," the gunslinger said in a lazy drawl. "I'm not wanting folks to know it was me."

"Why'd you come then?" Kent asked in surprise. The disguise—such as it was—had sure worked. Until Eli was right in front of him, he hadn't known who he was.

The gunslinger's gaze grew considering. "Figured since you hadn't come to us yet to tell your story, I'd come to you. Hurry things along."

Kent swallowed hard. There was no way to argue, though, as Eli sauntered through the door and back into the heat of the day. Kent followed, and as they passed the sheriff's office, prayed at the end of the day he wouldn't find himself in a jail cell.

It was one thing to play nice with Harry and buy time. They had history. He could twist his words, make them mean what Harry wanted to hear. But Kent was sure as the day was long he wouldn't be able to do the same with Eli Jones.

"Let's have a bite," Eli said, stopping at the diner door. "A little pie in the belly makes a sour story sweeter."

Kent followed him inside and to a back corner. Madge set down pie without asking, while Joy set down cups of water, and both women hurried away.

Tension filled every inch of him. But before he had time to get his thoughts and worries into any semblance of order, Eli spoke. "I know who you are, and I know why you're here."

His mouth suddenly parched, Kent nearly gulped down half his glass of water. "That so?" he asked.

"Yep. Not a soul comes to town that we don't learn about them." Eli picked up his fork, and slid it into the wedge of apple pie before him.

"I don't want trouble," Kent said, his voice low. "I promise. I just want to run my hotel."

"I know," Eli said. "It can be hard when your friends aren't the kind you can rely on to help you."

It was true. Kent hadn't ever had friends like that. For as long as he could remember—until he came here—he'd been running. It was hard to make friends when you were going place to place looking for work or some quick easy cash just to survive. Sometimes, he watched the gunslingers and their friends and felt a pang of longing for a friendship like they had.

Kent had been on his own since the uncle who'd raised him decided a boy of fourteen was old enough to take care of himself. That's when his problems had started, but he'd managed to do what many couldn't, and that was stop. Get out. Go straight.

What would his path have been like, if he'd had a friend or two, true ones, that he could have relied on?

He glanced at Eli, and then shook his head. "It's strange seeing you dressed like that."

"Feels a little odd," the gunslinger said. "Hannah laughed at me."

For some reason, that made Kent chuckle. "You're a lucky guy," he said.

"I am," Eli agreed. "A beautiful wife, three kids, and good friends." He was quiet a moment and said, "I'd like to count you as one of them."

"Me?" Kent asked, surprised. "But I'm...well, you know what I was. And what I'm trying to be."

"And here I am," Eli said mildly, taking a bite. "A gunslinger turned father and rancher. Same with Billy. Heck, Gavin's a lawman now. Doesn't mean we don't keep ourselves sharp, use our past—the good and the bad parts—to help take care of others."

"I'd like that," Kent said, "but how does a thief do that?"

"By doing what he does best," Eli said with a sly grin. "Picking a mark."

"I'm listening," Kent said, pulling his pie closer.

An hour later, Kent left the diner. He couldn't believe what had happened. What Eli had suggested. He'd need to think it over. He also couldn't stop the words ringing around in his head, that Eli wanted him as a friend.

What would that be like? Harry and Jimbo, working together for nearly a decade didn't have that kind of easy friendship with him that Kent suspected he might enjoy with the gunslinger. Kent very much doubted that Harry or Jimbo even trusted the other.

He'd gone his whole life without true friends. If Eli were one, and then the others, what would change? For one, he might not feel so alone, perhaps. He was going to have to think it over.

Kent neared the sheriff's office, intending to cross over to the hotel, when he saw Billy and Gavin glance around and stop at the corner of the building.

Not wanting to be seen, Kent froze. Their words carried easily to his ears, and he listened to what would be the answer to his prayers.

"When the private stage stops over for the night, we'll deliver the passenger safe to the hotel," Gavin said. "They're going to be carrying a lot of coin on them. I'll put a man outside the hotel. You think you can see the stage safe to the livery?"

"Sure can," Billy said. "You think one man is enough?"

"No one's going to be expecting a woman to have that much on her," Gavin said. "That's why we don't need but one."

"Can't imagine feeling safe traveling with thousands of dollars in coin with me," Billy said. "Too heavy. Nowhere to hide it."

Thousands of dollars. This was perfect. It was a big payday, and the kind of thing that would make Harry and Jimbo jump on it. He didn't know about Sam, but he was sure once the men had the money, they'd move on quickly.

And then, he'd be safe, his secret would be safe, but most importantly of all, Betty would be safe.

Chapter 14

It had been a busy afternoon in the store. Betty was glad it had quieted down. For a time, there had been chaos, and a woman who'd brought eggs to sell was knocked into by a man in a hurry. Her eggs had flown from the basket they'd been in, and landed on the floor, on the counter, and on a packet of coffee beans.

Betty had cleaned it all up, while her aunt, even though she didn't have to, paid the woman for the eggs, and decided the coffee beans would be for her and Betty's personal use.

As she stifled a yawn, Betty wondered when their shop window would be fixed. She hoped soon. Though, even if it was, would she ever feel a sense of security again in their cozy little home above? When she'd expressed that concern to her aunt, Aunt Glinda had thought for a time, and first, reassured her of the heavy wooden door between the shop and the living area, then offered to teach Betty how to shoot, just in case.

That was something Betty wasn't sure about. It might come in handy though, so she'd told her aunt she'd consider it.

Tiredly, she rubbed at her eyes. Perhaps just the knowledge that she could defend herself if needed would help her to get the sleep she knew she was missing. Besides, knowing how to do something and needing to do it were two very different things, but peace of mind was incredibly important.

Through the broken glass pane, Betty could see Gus walking closer. She fought back a smile. She bet he was going to stop in. He had come by multiple times to check on them, and Betty couldn't help but appreciate the old man's gesture.

As the door opened, she greeted him warmly. "Hello, Gus. How are you?"

He glanced around, presumably for her aunt. "Doing well, but got a question," he said, lowering his voice.

"Of course. What is it?" Betty asked.

"Reckon I was wondering. Glinda got a favorite sweet?"

Gus didn't quite look at her as he asked, and it was now all Betty could do not to swoon over how adorable he was being. However, she didn't want to embarrass the man, so instead, she nodded. Moving to a shelf behind the counter, she pulled down a flat box about the size of a book.

"Aunt Glinda adores these chocolates, but she rarely gets them for herself."

"That so?" Gus asked, bringing a hand to his face. "Well then, wontcha wrap 'em up for me? Make it all purdy like. I'm planning to give 'em to her before your store closes." He swallowed hard. "When I invite her for dinner at the hotel."

"That's a wonderful idea," Betty said. "I'll use our special paper."

She reached under the counter for a sheet of white paper and carefully wrapped the box of chocolates, and then tied a blue ribbon around it, making a neat bow.

"Fine, fine," Gus said, grinning at the package, and then at Betty. "Don't say nothing, now."

"Not a word," Betty promised.

After paying, Gus picked up the package and tucked it under his arm. Whistling cheerfully, he left the store. Betty scarcely had time to turn around when the store door opened.

When she glanced over, the smile fell from her lips. Harry, Jimbo, and Sam stood there. For a moment, Betty wasn't sure what she was supposed to do. Should she let on that she recognized Sam? Was he going to pretend he didn't know her? And, should she play along? Betty let out a tentative hello, and wished she weren't alone in the store.

How was it that these men always came in when she was alone? It made her wonder if they were watching the store and timed it as such.

"Well now, lookie here," Harry said. He sneered at Betty, though she wondered if he was actually trying to be flirtatious.

"Can I help you with something?" Betty asked, trying to ignore his action.

"Good to see you again, Betty," Sam said, leaning against the counter as though he came in frequently, and the last time he saw her hadn't been states away.

She decided to address it. "I never imagined seeing you here," Betty told him. "How-how are you?"

Betty hoped her nerves weren't showing. The awkward, frightened feeling she had just now.

"Doing fine, doing fine," Sam said, though he didn't elaborate or mention surprise at seeing her.

Should she ask why he was here? Ignore it? Betty had no idea, but wished she knew.

"I wonder, pretty girl," Harry said, also leaning against the counter, "if you knew what kind of a past Kenty boy had, if you'd still be so sweet on him."

"Maybe our girl likes men a little bit dangerous," Sam replied. "That's why she was always sweet on me."

"I'm—" Betty stopped. She couldn't truthfully deny that she was sweet on Kent. Or, that at one time, had been on Sam. But as for Kent's past...did that mean he was caught up with whatever trouble these three seemed to be up to? The idea made her heart start to hammer.

"You know," Sam said, and Betty flicked her eyes to him, "your sister...she's pretty and all, but I don't think it's going to work out between us. You, on the other hand, you're built of the better stuff. Practical, not demanding. Content with life. Maybe you'd be a better fit for me. What do you say? Then you can get the man you fell for first."

"I didn't fall for you," Betty whispered. "You are my sister's intended."

"Naw, not anymore," Sam said, holding a hand up to inspect his fingernails. "I wrote her a letter. Told her I got what I needed."

"What was that?" Betty asked, hoping desperately it wasn't anything to do with her.

"A place to hide for a while." Sam shrugged. "Though she didn't need to know that. Just like Harry and Jimbo came here for. Nope. But it would have been fun to see what your parents thought I meant. I suspect they worry her reputation was ruined."

She looked for Jimbo, who had been quiet, and still was. When she spotted him, arms across his chest and standing in front of the general store door, almost blocking it, Betty wet her lips nervously.

"And, Kent, of course," Sam continued. That brought Betty's attention back to him. "Though, I hadn't ever met him. Was just coincidence he was here when we arrived. As it was with you."

Betty would have liked to relax slightly, now that she knew it was pure chance that Sam's path had crossed with her own, but she still felt on edge. Worry was filling her at the idea Kent was mixed up with these people. She longed to see him, to ask what was going on, but at the same time, she was scared, and wondered if she did go to him, if what he'd tell her would be nothing but lies.

"What do you say, Betty?" Sam asked. He reached for her, but Betty stepped backward, to the laughter of Harry. Sam's eyes hadn't left hers. "I've moved on from your sister. But you...I'd play house with you if you want. I'm not promising anything but a little fun, but I promise you'll have it."

"Please leave," Betty said firmly. Well, as firmly as she could with her voice trembling. "Now."

"Of course," Sam answered, acting the perfect gentleman. "I'll see you soon."

Betty didn't answer. She only watched as Jimbo opened the door, and he, Sam, and Harry left the store.

Worry filled her. What to do? Could anything be done? Betty started toward the shop door. There! One of the Miller children was crossing over.

"Psst! Jimmy!" she whispered, and waved at him.

The boy, about ten, drew closer. "Whatcha need, Miss Betty?" he asked.

"I'll give you a nickel and a candy stick if you take a note to the sheriff for me. You have to see he gets it though."

"Okay. Say, can I get a green one?" Jimmy asked.

"Yes, here," Betty said, hurriedly handing him the candy and the nickel from the register. "Just a moment. I need to write it."

Taking up a piece of paper, Betty thought for a moment, then wrote:

Gavin, I think those men from the hotel are up to something. They've tried to imply that Kent is as well. I don't know if that's true or not, but I do know I'm scared.

"Here, now, straight over and give it right to the sheriff," Betty reminded.

"Okay, Miss Betty," Jimmy answered, and left, the stick of candy in his mouth.

Betty waited impatiently. She was anxious for the store to close. She decided she'd make her way to the hotel and look for Kent. They had to talk. It didn't matter what her heart felt. If Kent was in danger or he was the danger, she needed to act. The gunslingers weren't the only ones wanting to protect their town.

Chapter 15

"Tell me again," Harry ordered as he paced the room. "Nice and slow."

Kent nodded. "Just after sundown, a stage arrives. On it is the wife of a land baron. Her escorts took sick, so she'll be staying at the hotel alone. She's got a few thousand dollars on her, and for safekeeping will have it in a travel bag."

"Something don't smell right," Sam said. "The sheriff told you this why?"

"He only told me the part about her staying here," Kent replied impatiently. "I own the hotel, so he needed to ensure her safety. The rest—about the money—I overheard, and they didn't know I was listening in. How many times do I have to tell you that?"

"Told you we had nothing to worry about with Kenty boy," Harry said, shooting a triumphant look toward

Jimbo and Sam. "Now, you boys all know your part in the plan?"

"Sure do," Jimbo said.

"Looking forward to it," Sam answered in a tone that Kent didn't like.

He also didn't hesitate to call him out on it. "Not sure I trust the sound of that," he said with a frown.

"Not sure I care," Sam said. "You ain't part of us no more, so you don't need to know all our doings."

Kent knew that Sam was right, and he'd been fortunate to hear as much of the plan so far as he had. But something still set the tiny hairs on his neck to raising, and a feeling of warning filled him.

"You make sure the horses are ready," Harry ordered Jimbo.

"Already have," Jimbo answered. "Done told you that each time you asked."

Harry just grunted and sat in a chair. He picked at the leftover crumbs on a tray of food that had been brought in a few hours earlier. "Now all we do is wait," he said.

Kent nodded. "I need to get about my duties," he said.

"Duties," Sam sneered. "Listen to you talking like you're better than the rest of us."

The words "I am" nearly burst from Kent, but he stopped himself just in time. "It's my hotel," he said instead, mildly. "If I'm holed up here, it's sure going to draw a little attention your way."

"Don't worry about him," Harry said to Sam. "We got our plan to ensure his cooperation."

Though Sam nodded, Kent didn't miss his scowl, or how his eyes narrowed. As the words took a moment to spin through his head and settle between his ears, Kent froze, his hand hovering above the doorknob. "What do you mean? Ensure my cooperation?"

"That's for me to know, and you to worry about." Sam smirked.

Kent dropped his hand. "You know, I don't know why you seem to hate me so much," he said.

"A man needs a reason?" Sam asked.

"When he's living under another man's roof, eating his food, living in his town, then yeah. Either settle up and pay your bill, or get out. I never did anything to you."

Kent opened the door and shook his head. "When you go, make sure you don't come back. If you do, I won't bother with doing things legal. I'll shoot you myself."

While Harry and Jimbo hooted and slapped their knees, Sam growled. Kent shut the door and hurried to the front desk. He needed to make sure everything was according to plan.

Clyde looked up as he approached. "Sir?"

"Just wanted to be sure the suite was ready for our guest," he said.

There weren't any suites open, so he'd planned to put the woman traveler on the second floor. Harry hadn't liked that; it would take longer for them to get away. So, he said, since they'd be leaving right after they stole the money, they'd move into the room on the second floor, and let the woman have the suite.

Harry, Jimbo, and Sam had wandered out while the suite was cleaned and their new room made ready. Kent had noticed they went into Mrs. Stover's store. They didn't stay too long, for which he was grateful, but he also hoped that they hadn't been bothering Betty. With any luck, she wasn't there.

"Mr. Jackson? The chef needs you," a waitress called from the dining room doors.

"Be right there," Kent said. He suppressed a sigh, and headed to see what crisis there was now. All he wanted was for the day to be over, the deed to be done, and his "guests" to be gone.

He really hoped, too, that at the end of the day, when everything was done, Betty would understand why he'd done what he had, and she wouldn't hold it against him too harshly. For the first time in his life, he'd come across someone who made his breath catch, his heart pound, and his desire grow to be a better man—not just for himself, but for everyone. He just hoped he wasn't making a mistake.

Chapter 16

Closing time. Finally. All afternoon, Betty had been anxious for the hour to come when she could lock up and seek out Kent.

She'd gone from thinking he was a criminal to feeling confident about Harry lying. But then, there was the whole issue with Sam. How he'd teased her. Offered to...

"I would never," Betty said, wondering how her sister felt right now. If she even knew. A part of Betty was glad knowing that Sam would never be part of her family, and not just because at one time, she'd been attracted to him. No, her family didn't need a man such as him in it. Dishonest in multiple ways.

The other part of her, however, felt terrible for her sister. When she found out, would she cry? Scream? Maybe she'd move on, easily and without it bothering her much. Perhaps the real question was, would their mother?

There were so many questions her head was starting to ache. Then, there was the reply from the sheriff. Gavin had answered her message quickly. It had been short and to the point. It had simply said:

Don't worry.

Don't worry? How like a man to say not to worry, and without giving any reasons as to *why* she shouldn't worry. The words were enough to make her fume, and she'd added that to the list of things bothering her.

Betty was just switching the sign on the general store door from open to closed when she saw Kent rushing over across the street. She paused, wondering if he was heading her direction. Then her heart beat a little faster as she saw he was.

Quickly, she unlocked the door, and held it open for him as he came in. "Thank you," he said, as he glanced at the wood nailed over the broken window. "I am glad you have a temporary fix."

"I am as well," Betty told him. "And, I'm glad to see you. I was about to come and look for you at the hotel."

"You were? I've got to speak with you urgently," Kent said. "I don't have a lot of time."

"It sounds important," Betty said. "Do you want to sit? We have some chairs near the side over here. They're for sale, but Aunt Glinda won't mind."

"As much as I'd love to, and I'd like to stay for a while, I can't. I..." Kent drew in a deep breath and closed his eyes briefly, as though he was steeling himself. When he refocused his attention on her, his voice was low. Serious.

"Betty, you may hear things about me. You might have already heard things about me. No matter what you've heard, I'm not a bad person."

"I have," Betty said slowly. "And that's why I wanted to see you. I heard some things. But I'm feeling confused."

"How I wish I had the time to sort everything out. To tell you everything. But I can't. The sun will set soon, and..." Kent ran his fingers through his hair.

"Are you sure you can't tell me about what's upset you so much? What does the sun have to do with anything?" Betty asked.

"Tomorrow, I hope, I'll be able to tell you," Kent said. "It's all part of the reason why I've not stopped by sooner. To keep you safe."

He reached for her hand, and Betty let him take it. Warm fingers, slightly rough, closed around hers. They felt nice. He felt nice. Betty was glad to see him. She just wished she knew what was upsetting him so. She was relieved to have learned the reason he'd not stopped by, other than being busy, even if it was worrying to hear.

What did he want to protect her from? Harry, and Jimbo, and Sam had been here, so it couldn't have been them, could it?

"I'll be here," Betty said. "I want to hear whatever it is you have to say. I…I didn't want to think badly of you, and I don't. But, Kent, I admit, I'm very confused."

"I don't blame you," Kent told her with a sigh. "And I've promised to keep quiet for now. It's a promise I have to keep. The short of it is, I made mistakes in my past and came here to start over. However, some of those mistakes found me. Please believe me, I don't want anyone hurt. I'm trying to do the best I can to set things right."

Betty trembled. His past. Harry had spoken of such a thing. So, there must have been truth in his words to her earlier. Distress filled her. Kent must have realized it, for he squeezed her hands. He looked as though he wanted to say something, but she spoke before he could.

"You are scaring me. Whatever it is that's happening, let me help. Or, at least let me get the sheriff to help," Betty pleaded. "You don't have to do whatever you seem like you are going to do alone."

"I don't ever want to scare you. I like you. More than like you. I know I don't deserve a woman such as you. Not as a friend, not as anything more. When I have the chance to explain everything, I'll understand if you never talk to me again."

"That sounds so drastic," Betty said. "Don't I get any say?"

He hesitated. "You'd consider having feelings for someone who might have a black past?"

"No," Betty said, shaking her head. "But I'd consider having feelings for you."

"Betty, I don't know what to say," Kent said.

"You'll just have to get over that," she teased. "I belong to you. That is," her cheeks warmed, "if you want me."

"I do, more than anything," Kent whispered. "I just hope tomorrow, you'll feel the same as you do right now. Tomorrow, everything could change. Or it could have gone very wrong."

She didn't like hearing that, and longed to ease some of the strain in his voice and tension throughout his body.

"Just in case I don't," Betty said, in her own whisper, even though she had no doubt in her mind she would, "let me kiss you one more time."

Kent's lips had barely pressed to Betty's, her world starting to spin all around her, when the general store door opened. They startled, both jumping backward, and then Betty shrieked as Harry walked in, a gun pointed at her.

Chapter 17

Kent tried to push Betty behind him, but Sam had moved with faster speed than he'd have imagined, and had wrapped his arm around Betty's neck, a knife at it.

"Hello, you two." Sam laughed, and it was a cruel, vile thing that Kent knew would remain in his ears for however many minutes he had left to live. His life, however, didn't matter to him. Betty's did.

"I told you to stay away from her," he growled, wanting to move toward her, but scared Sam would hurt her if he did. Perhaps he could appeal to his reason. "Aren't I helping you? In trade—"

"In trade nothing," Jimbo said. "We don't take orders from you. Only Harry. And he's making sure we buy your cooperation."

"That's right," Harry said, shoving the barrel of the gun into Kent's gut. "Sun's almost down. Time to go, lover boy. You know what you have to do."

"No," Betty whispered. "You don't have to, Kent. Whatever it is, you don't have to get caught up in it."

"I do," Kent said softly, his eyes searching her face, and lingering on the tears that tracked down her cheeks. "It's the only way to be sure you are safe."

"That's not important," Betty said. "Staying true to yourself is. And this isn't you. You aren't that kind of person."

"Aww, listen to them," Sam said sarcastically. "Let's go. This is making me sick to my stomach."

Jimbo opened the door, and stuck his head out. "All clear."

Kent let himself be shoved into the street. Betty was there as well. He didn't know why he'd hoped they'd leave her behind in the store. This was worse. Would she be forced to watch him? Misunderstand what was happening?

Or, would the unthinkable happen? And one of them die before the other? Sam had wrapped an arm around her waist and had a revolver shoved into her side. Kent's eyes were flicking through the town. How was it no one was outside right now? Usually, there were at least a few people this time of day in the streets.

Carefully, Kent weighed the chances of driving his shoulder and elbow just so, and knocking the gun away from Harry. Even taking it for his own. But his former associate seemed to know just what he was thinking.

"Don't try it," Harry warned. "We'll kill her, straight away, and the blood will be on your hands. In more ways than one."

"So this was your plan all along?" Kent growled, as he was pushed toward the hotel. "Taking Betty?"

"Naw, it weren't," Jimbo said. "But Sam thought of it, and it's real good, isn't it? Will make sure you do what you're supposed to do."

Kent shot a glance at Betty. Her face was so pale, and her eyes so frightened, he knew the sight would haunt him forever. Still, she tried to smile, and look brave. That was just as hard for him to see.

It felt like he'd been stabbed in the heart, and punched in the gut at the same time. He hadn't trusted Harry, not at all, but he'd never thought the man would stoop so low.

"Betty has nothing to do with this," Kent said, his voice low as he was pushed into the hotel lobby, and prayed none of the guests crossed their paths.

Quiet voices trickled from the restaurant, as did the piano music that played softly. Thankfully, all appeared well, and no one seemed to notice the strange way they were clustered together, or the weapons pointed at him and Betty. Kent was sure things would go very wrong if it was noticed.

The night manager Paul glanced up from the check-in desk, but Kent gave the smallest shake of his head. The man quickly looked down, flipping the page of the book before him. It was all Kent could do to hope Jimbo wouldn't go after the man. He was glad the manager had seemed to understand, but wondered just what he might be thinking.

Thankfully, no one but him seemed to have noticed Paul glancing their way, and Kent relaxed—as much as one could with a gun in their back—and led the way to the room Harry, Jimbo, and Sam had claimed until the stagecoach arrived and they left.

Once the door opened, Sam pushed Betty into the room. "I'll tie her," he said. "Where's the rope?"

Jimbo handed it over, and Kent watched, every bit of him wanting to fight the three men as Betty's hands were tied, and then her legs, to the chair in the corner.

"Let's go," Harry said, pushing Kent toward the door.

"Betty," Kent whispered. "I'm sorry. I didn't mean—"

"Shesh it," Jimbo said, and blew out the lantern, leaving her in the near darkness.

The door closed behind them, and the last glimpse of Betty nearly made Kent's heart stop. She was looking at him so sadly, he could only imagine what she was thinking. Likely how he was a liar. How, if he didn't die tonight, she'd finish the job. She was disappointed in him, and that might be the worst feeling he'd ever had in his life.

"I should have known better," Kent whispered.

"What's that?" Harry asked with a frown.

"Said, I should have known better," Kent said. There was no need to fake the regret in his voice. "About letting myself fall for a woman. Knowing it could be used against me."

What he wasn't saying was the part about how he also should have known better about Harry and Jimbo. How he should have gone to the sheriff right away. Not think he could handle things on his own. He couldn't. And Harry had known it. Might have even had Betty as his backup plan to make Kent go along with whatever he'd wanted the whole time.

"That's all right," Harry said kindly, and patted him on the shoulder, though his gun hand never wavered. "Sometimes takes a lesson to remember the only thing you can count on is cold, hard cash."

There were grunts of agreement from Jimbo and Sam. Kent nodded his head in agreement, but what he was really thinking was that no, there was so much more.

There was friendship, if one sought it. There were also a good number of people out there who were honest. Who put themselves in the path for others, to protect them.

Kent swallowed hard. Red Ridge was full of those sorts of folks, but he hadn't made things go well for them, inviting in the likes of Harry and Jimbo to his hotel. When word got out about what he'd done...

"Now what?" Jimbo asked. "I done forgot."

Three sets of eyes came to him, and Kent said, "We watch for the stage. We can use this window here. It's overlooking the livery. Shouldn't be much longer. The woman will get out, and be escorted by the sheriff."

"Then," Harry said, taking up the plan, "the woman gets to her room. We wait a half hour for her to settle in. That's when Kenty boy here will knock at the door. Tell her he's got her dinner."

"Wouldn't it look less suspicious if I actually had the meal on a tray?" Kent asked. "What if she opens the door a crack to be sure? A woman traveling alone might just do that, and scream if she thinks I'm lying."

"Got a point," Harry muttered.

"What? No! So you can tell them in the kitchen what's going on?" Sam protested.

"No, so that it looks more real," Kent snapped. "Use your head, boy."

"Kent's right," Harry said. "So, he and I will go to the kitchen, get the food once the woman's in her room. You boys stay here."

"Remember," Sam hissed, "anything goes wrong, we kill the girl."

Kent fixed Sam with the angriest look he thought he'd ever given. "It won't. Everything's going according to plan."

And he sure hoped every word of that was true because when he'd agreed to do this, he had no idea Betty was going to be here, and Kent was desperate to save her life. It didn't matter that she'd spend the rest of her days hating him. He wanted to make sure she had days, not minutes. It was the only way he could show his love.

Chapter 18

Betty tried to wriggle her wrists, but somehow it made the ropes even tighter. When Sam had tied her to the chair, he hadn't been gentle. In fact, the way he'd smirked led her to believe he was taking pleasure in treating her so roughly.

The chafing at her wrists was growing numb, and her fingers had long since felt heavy and painful. Being numb as the blood flow was cut off would almost be welcome.

There was nothing she could do but sit here, try and get herself free, and worry. Ah, the worry. Betty had a lot of that right now. Everything had happened so quickly. She'd felt something was wrong, had worried so much about it. And then...it had happened.

Perhaps the worst part of this all, though, was the fact that Kent was involved, and he seemed to be doing it, thinking it was because it was a way to protect her. Betty would much rather he let her take her chances than to get caught up with criminals. Or have him entangled with them. This must have been what he was trying to tell her.

The look on his face...the pain, the worry... Betty swallowed hard, and fought back the tightness in her throat. The lump that had been there since she'd been forced to walk to the hotel. She'd never be able to forget the sorry and regret Kent wore, and how his shoulders had slumped as he appeared to turn inward.

Harry and Sam had seemed to take delight in it. Jimbo had seemed impassive, but that didn't mean the man was an ally. Far from it. She sensed he'd have been willing to step in and hurt one of them if asked.

But all was not lost. Not if she could escape. There was a window, and she could open it, call for help, or even swing down from the curtains. She'd figure out that part when she got to it, but she couldn't do that until she got her hands free.

The last of the sunset had gone, and she was in the dark. She wished the lantern hadn't been blown out, and assumed that was done so that it would be more difficult for her to escape. At the very least, it had prevented her from looking around the room in search of an object to help free her bonds.

It was odd to her they hadn't gagged her mouth, though she was immensely grateful for that. For a moment, Betty thought about screaming, but worried if she did call for help, Kent would be shot. She wouldn't put it past any of the men to do so.

That was if Kent wasn't willingly going along with them.

The idea made her shiver. Betty hoped she was right in her first instinct, and that Kent wasn't a willing participant in whatever crime was about to happen.

Betty's hands were growing numb. While that eased the pain, it made moving her hands even more difficult. She tried again to loosen the ropes that cut into her, but it was hopeless.

Think! She ordered herself. *There must be something you can do. Figure it out.*

She tried to recall what the room had looked like when she was pushed in, and in the short glance she'd had before the lantern was blown out. There was a table, some dishes... It was pointless. She'd been so focused on the weapon on her, and on Kent's face, she'd failed to observe much else.

Fine. Another plan then. One that didn't require her ropes untied.

She'd just had the idea to throw herself forward and try and crawl best as she could toward the window or door, when there was a thump outside the window.

Betty froze. They were on the second floor. So, what could that sound have been? She squeezed her eyes shut and whispered a prayer. The noise continued, then she felt a rush of wind as the window opened and a breeze washed over her face.

What was happening?

Every inch of her more scared than she'd been, she held as still as she could, and willed the trembling that started in her core and spread outward to stop.

There was a rustling sound, and the feeling she was no longer alone. Betty forced herself to look, but the moon wasn't at the right angle, and she couldn't see anything. Should she keep quiet? Scream out? Betty wasn't sure, but she was certain that she'd never been so frightened. Or so aware that her days on earth were very limited.

Shadows entered the room, and then someone whispered, "Light."

A soft light from a small lantern illuminated, but it wasn't enough for Betty to see much. She couldn't help it; a gasp tore from her, and she pleaded, "Don't kill me!"

"I'm not going to kill you," a gentle and familiar voice said.

Betty cracked one eyelid open, and then cried out softly. But this time in relief.

"Shh," Eli said, his voice low, bending over with a small knife he used to saw at the ropes on her arms. "You hurt?"

"Not much," Betty answered, fighting back the urge to throw her arms around him, she was so grateful to see the gunslinger.

"Anything you can tell us that will help?" Gavin asked from his position just inside the door.

Betty glanced around to see if anyone else was with them, but even though there wasn't, she felt much better now. Though she'd never seen the gunslingers in action, she knew the stories about them weren't boasts. If anyone could help, it would be these two.

"There are three men, Harry, Jimbo, and Sam." Betty said, rubbing her wrists while Eli cut the ropes around her feet. "They've got guns and knives. And..." she gulped, "and Kent. He's there too. But I don't think he has a weapon. They, they..." She stopped. What should she say? Admit they were all working together?

"They headed to the suite?" Eli asked.

Betty wiggled her ankles to get the blood back in them. "I don't rightly know," she admitted. "I only know that there was something about sundown, and he was helping them in trade for my protection."

"Seems his friends went back on their end," Eli said dryly.

"Kent, he's a good man," Betty started.

"Don't you be worrying," Gavin said, and shot her a rare grin after he interrupted. "Everything's going according to plan."

To plan? Whose? Theirs?

Betty glanced between the two men. Gavin was easing the door open, and had one of his revolvers in his hand. Eli had one as well. When had he taken it from his gunbelt? She wasn't sure.

"Stay here," Eli whispered. "Don't make any sounds. You'll be safe though, I promise. We won't let anyone past us."

She wanted to protest. To argue. Offer to help in some way. But both gunslingers were out the door, and it closed behind them so quickly that had it not been for the curtains blowing in the breeze, and the fact she was now untied, Betty might have thought she was imagining things.

Chapter 19

He had to stay calm. Play along. It was the only way to keep Betty safe. Kent kept repeating those words to himself as he passed through the hotel lobby, Harry at his back, and into the restaurant. Kent smiled, nodded, and greeted the guests who were still there, much to Harry's discomfort, but he knew the man understood. This was his job. As he owned the hotel and the restaurant, this behavior was expected.

As Kent pushed open the door to the kitchen, he spotted a tray being filled. "Is this for our special guest?" he asked the chef.

"It is, sir," the chef answered, as he glanced at Harry curiously.

Kent didn't let on that he was disturbed in any way. "Thank you," he said. "I'll carry it to her."

"I just need to add the pie," the chef said, hurrying away to a long table that had precut desserts on it. He picked up a slice of strawberry pie, with fat juicy berries spilling out of the golden crust, and set it carefully on the tray. After adding a white linen napkin, along with a knife, fork, and spoon, the chef stepped back.

Kent took the tray, a little surprised by the weight. As he didn't do this often, each time he carried one he felt a new appreciation for the staff who worked here and did this daily. It took a great deal of effort to make sure none of the dishes or the hot tea slid around. His staff made it look effortless.

Once he got out of this, he'd remember to tell them how fine of a job they did.

"You'll need to get the door," Kent said to Harry, worried if he raised his eyes from the tray he might tip it.

Harry hurried in front of him, seemingly not concerned Kent might try anything. For the briefest of moments, Kent wondered what would happen if he threw the tray at his former associate. Would that buy enough time to wrestle the man down?

But if he went to the suite without Harry, Jimbo and Sam would know he'd done something, so Kent went along with their plan.

For now.

He knew what their plan was. They'd been talking about it since he first told them about the stagecoach.

However, after Betty had been taken prisoner, Kent knew that Harry didn't have a problem with changing the plan, with or without consulting anyone else.

He'd always been a bit like that, Kent reflected, as he walked down the hallway nearing the suite. A stick of dynamite with a lit match nearby. It made him dangerous.

Before him, he could see Jimbo and Sam, both eagerly waiting.

"She's inside," Jimbo whispered loudly. "Sheriff brought her and left."

"What's she look like?" Harry asked.

"Don't know. She had one of those veils on, like some people wear for the dust," Jimbo said.

"Or to hide the uglies," Sam laughed, not trying to be quiet.

"She alone?" Harry pressed.

"Just her and that beautiful bag of money." Jimbo grinned. "Let's hurry up."

"Can you knock for me?" Kent asked. "This tray is getting wobbly."

"Weakling," Sam snorted, but raised his hand and knocked.

"Madam? I'm the hotel owner, and here with your dinner," Kent called.

There was a long pause, but they heard the lock snick open. The plan was to wait and let Kent set the tray down, see the woman seated, and then the others would rush in. Kent hoped they'd stick to that part, at least.

When the door opened, Kent saw the veiled woman. He carefully balanced the tray and brought it into her room. As he slid it onto the table, he said, "If you need anything, there's a bell pull by the door. Simply ring it, and myself or the night manager will come."

The woman inclined her head, and moved to take a seat. It was then that Harry, Jimbo, and Sam rushed into the room.

"Gimmie yer bag," Harry snarled.

The woman didn't move.

"You deaf?" Jimbo asked. "Where is it?"

The woman raised a gloved hand, and pointed. A whisper so faint Kent could hardly hear it said, "Over there."

Four pairs of eyes looked where she pointed, Kent's included. Sure enough, tucked in the corner of the room was a travel case, near bulging.

Harry and Sam went toward it, while Jimbo stood grinning. "Oh boy, oh boy," he said, rubbing his hands together.

Just then, there was the sound of guns cocking. Kent looked back at the woman, and it was all he could do not to laugh.

She had raised her veil, and in each hand was a revolver. But instead of the guest being a woman, it was none other than Billy Madison, a calm expression on his face, along with the hint of a smirk, as he said, "Hands up."

Kent wasn't sure who was more surprised to see the gunslinger, but he wasn't going to let the element of surprise go to waste. The moment he grabbed Sam and pulled him backward, an arm around his neck just like the man had done to Betty earlier, the suite door burst open and Eli and Gavin were there, guns out.

"Looks like you're outgunned," Billy said, rising from the chair.

"You ain't no woman!" Jimbo howled in shock.

"No, I'm sure not," Billy said with a laugh. "And you weren't smart enough to see that, huh?"

"Yeah, well, we got ourselves an insurance policy," Harry said, his smirk returning. "And if you want her alive, you're gonna back away from the loot right now and let us leave." He tossed a look toward Sam and shrugged, "But you can have him, Kenty boy. I don't care."

Sam started to sputter in rage, but Kent kept his grip. "Much obliged," he replied. "But I can't let any of you leave. I should have been firmer when you first came. Not let the past sway me, nor my fear of the future."

"While you keep talking, I'll just let myself out," Harry said. He grabbed the bag by the handle, and started to heft it.

"There's no money in there," the sheriff said, his voice full of humor.

"There ain't?" Jimbo asked.

"Boys, do you really think we'd set up the whole thing and actually give you real money?" Eli asked. He raised his brows and said to Kent, "They're even stupider than I thought."

"That doesn't change the fact of our insurance policy," Harry said, anger flashing in his eyes now. "You want Betty alive, you let us go."

Before anyone could say another word, Harry had flung himself at the suite door, and gotten out, shutting the door behind him.

There was a flurry of activity as Jimbo tried to follow, but Billy—still dressed as a woman—lunged forward with a punch. He missed, but Eli didn't, and jammed an elbow into Jimbo's gut, then landed a solid punch across his jaw that knocked him out.

"I coulda done it," Billy muttered, "if it weren't for this dress. It's a mite confining. Don't know how the ladies tolerate it."

Sam struggled, kicking out with his feet. Kent forced him toward Billy and Eli, who grabbed him and had him tied faster than Kent would have thought possible, and lying face down on the rug.

"Shooting would have been faster," Kent said, "but I sure appreciate you trying to be quiet because of the hotel guests."

"I'll take care of him," Billy said, as he walked over to the dinner tray that had been untouched, though he kept a gun in one hand. "I reckon you want to go after the other one, and I sure don't want this pie to go to waste. I've got to get this dress off too. Hard to move in it."

That's right. Harry had gotten away. Kent tensed. There were two places Harry would have gone. To the livery, or to the room he'd locked Betty in. Without saying anything, Kent raced out of the suite, and toward the stairs.

"Betty's okay," Eli said, "we cut the ropes off her. She's supposed to be staying in the room. Hopefully, with the door locked. Gavin went right after Harry, so surely he didn't get to her."

Kent hoped he was right, but Betty was his responsibility. If something happened to her, he'd never be able to stop blaming himself.

He took the stairs in twos and caught his foot on the top one. As he stumbled forward, he found the hotel room Betty had been held in. The door was ajar.

There was no use calling out for her. She wasn't there. That meant one of two things. Harry already had her, or else she'd escaped. The best thing he could do now was go after Harry.

"The livery," Kent said, and flew down the stairs.

He took a side door few knew about, and it spit him a few feet away from the livery. There, his heart nearly stopped and fear filled every inch of him as he saw Harry, an arm around Betty, and a wild look in his eyes.

"Get away! I'm warning you!" he shouted.

Kent slowly walked closer. He could see Gavin waiting patiently. "Why didn't you do something?" he asked the sheriff, starting to get angry. "You're just standing there."

"Well now, I could shoot him, save the girl, save the day," Gavin answered calmly, "but I thought I'd just hold him here, let you do that. After all, she's yours, isn't she?"

"That's right, she is," Kent said, as gratitude and a little bit of embarrassment washed over him. He straightened a little taller. "I appreciate it."

He wasn't sure Betty had seen him yet. It was dark out, and he was well in the shadows. Betty was kicking out with her feet and flailing with her elbows. He watched as Harry took a few solid elbow strikes, but his old acquaintance wasn't releasing her.

"Harry!" Kent called loudly. "Let her go."

"Not a chance," Harry said.

Betty had stilled. She must have heard him. Kent took a step closer.

"No further," Harry said, backing up toward a horse. "I got a knife. I'll use it before you can stop me."

"I know you will," Kent answered, his voice calm. The air felt heavy. Time seemed to slow as regret weighed on him. "I told you, Harry. I put all that, all this, behind me. The past is the past. I'm a new man now. I've gone straight, and I've found a town where the men fight for the women they love, and the safety of the town. I can't let you jeopardize that."

"Big words for a man who doesn't hold any of the cards," Harry boasted.

He was at the horse now, and with a length of rope was starting to wind it around Betty.

"Got something better than cards," Kent answered. "Got that pocket knife you gave me back in San Bernardino. It's the only thing I kept from our days together, and I'm gonna return it."

Kent felt the weight of the knife in his fingers, but without regret, without hesitation, flicked his wrist and let it fly. Though he hadn't practiced throwing for years, his hand knew just what to do. The blade glided through the air and embedded itself right into Harry's leg.

Chapter 20

Betty wasn't exactly sure what had happened. One moment, she was there in the hotel room, her mouth agape as the gunslingers slipped through the door and closed it gently behind themselves. Then, she found herself creeping down the hallway after them.

She hadn't gone immediately because Betty knew without a doubt they would have heard her and sent her back to the room. Maybe even retied her to keep her from getting hurt, but her fear over what might happen to Kent fueled her courage and her determination.

The fact that she wasn't sure what to do now that she knew he was aiding criminals—had seemed to return to his past ways—would have to wait. First, she'd make sure he was okay. Then, she'd let her heart break when she told him goodbye. She couldn't be part of that life.

And now, as she was being pulled toward the livery by Harry, she felt that decision sorely in her bones. Any chance of escape was futile, and she regretted her hasty and heedless actions. Eli and the sheriff had things under control. Why had she thought she could help? She'd put herself in even more danger, and now, Gavin too.

"Let her go," the sheriff called.

Harry didn't answer, just twisted her arm behind her back. It was so painful, Betty cried out, and tears blurred her vision. He half dragged her to three horses saddled and hitched outside, and she lost sight of Gavin as a horse's belly blocked her line of sight.

Harry pushed her toward a large bay. "Git on," he snapped at her. "Hurry."

"I won't!" she cried out, trying to put distance between herself and the criminal.

"You should have stayed where I put you," Harry said, lunging forward and grabbing her arm again. He forced her closer to the horse. "Brought this on yourself."

It was true. She had stood on the hotel stairs, pressed against the wall and hoping no one saw her while she'd watched. Luckily, Eli and Gavin were focused on a suite's door. Gavin had his ear pressed to it, and was making some sort of hand signal Eli apparently understood.

Try though she might, Betty couldn't hear anything. It was unexpected when, seconds later, Gavin and Eli had burst into the room. There was the faint sound of a scuffle, and Harry scrambled into the hallway and ran toward the lobby as if his life depended on it. Looking back now, it probably had.

There had been only one thing on Betty's mind in that instant. Chasing after him and putting a stop to whatever it was he was planning to do.

How foolish she'd been. The moment Betty had stepped out of the hotel and into the night, dark shadows wrapped around her, making it difficult to see. That's when Harry had grabbed her.

"You don't want to do this," the sheriff warned. "Let her go."

"Can't do that. She's the thing that's going to get me out alive," Harry said. Then, more to himself, he muttered, "Can't trust nobody." He added, louder now, "I don't know what you've done with Jimbo and Sam, but you're not catching me."

"Harry!" Kent called loudly. "Let her go."

"Not a chance," Harry said.

Betty stilled. Kent was here, and she didn't want to risk anything happening to him, or her being a distraction. It might be the end of the two of them, but that didn't mean she wanted to see him hurt. Kent took a step closer.

"No further," Harry said, backing up toward a horse. "I got a knife. I'll use it before you can stop me." Betty didn't doubt that he had one. It might even be the same that Sam had held to her. She was scared to move but also scared not to. What should she do?

"I know you will," Kent answered. "I told you, Harry. I put all that, all this, behind me. The past is the past. I'm a new man now. I've gone straight, and I've found a town where the men fight for the women they love, and the safety of the town. I can't let you jeopardize that."

Did he mean that? Or was it just for her benefit? Betty wasn't sure, but didn't know if she could trust him.

"Big words for a man who doesn't hold any of the cards," Harry boasted.

He was at the horse now, and with a length of rope was starting to wind it around Betty. She pulled back, trying to get away from him.

"Got something better than cards," Kent called out. That was enough to make Harry pause. "Got that pocket knife you gave me back in San Bernardino. It's the only thing I kept from our days together, and I'm gonna return it."

Before she could figure out just what Kent meant, Harry howled in pain and Betty saw her chance. Harry shifted, reaching downward, and Betty pushed him away as hard as she could.

But he didn't go far.

Kent sprinted toward them, closing the distance faster than Betty would have imagined possible. The two men were suddenly a jumble of fists and grunts, as each tried to wrestle the other into submission.

She stood there, unsure what to do. Eli, Gavin, and now Billy stood watching, guns in hand but not making any effort to stop the fight. Betty was terrified Kent would get hurt and turned to the gunslingers, pleading, "Won't you do something?"

But at that moment, Kent hauled Harry up, glanced around, and when he spotted Gavin, asked, "Got a free jail cell?"

"Sure do," the sheriff answered. "Let's toss him in with the others."

The others. That must mean that Jimbo and Sam had been locked up too.

Betty wasn't quite sure what to do now. Should she run after Kent? See for herself how injured he was? But before she puzzled that thought out, Kent reappeared, standing under the lantern at the livery, and wearing the worried look she'd gotten far too used to seeing clouding his face. Now that the danger was passed, would the smile she loved to see return? But did it even matter? She couldn't be with him.

"Are you hurt?" Kent asked. "But before she could answer, he rushed to say, "I'm so sorry. I tried to make them leave. I just wanted to keep you safe."

She swallowed hard. "By stealing from a defenseless woman? Helping them to rob her?"

"It wasn't like that," Kent said.

"That's sure how it looked," Betty said, the disappointment finally pouring out of her. "I was so worried about you, but now that I know you've not left your past behind, that you're able to be tempted when old friends come around, I'm not sure your paying me a call in the future is a good idea."

The words had been so hard to say, but Betty had to do it. Had to be clear. Stand firm. Even if it was breaking her heart. Was Sam right? She liked men with a black past?

"Will you let me explain?" Kent asked.

"I'm not sure I want to hear your excuses," Betty told him.

"She wasn't defenseless," Kent said, his tone almost argumentative.

"That's right," Billy said, and Betty glanced over to see him leaning against the side of the livery. "No one's ever called me that."

"Not and not regretted it," Eli snorted.

Betty's confusion warred with her hurt. "I don't understand," she said. "I also don't know if I want to hear excuses."

"Let me explain?" Kent asked. "Please?"

Betty's head swiveled between the men as she considered his request. Reluctantly, she nodded and crossed her arms over her chest. "Fine."

Taking a deep breath, Kent started telling her just what had happened. The whole tale was incredible, and she shook her head as though to try to bring order to the chaos whirling inside of it.

"Wait!" Betty finally broke in. "Do you mean to tell me Billy disguised himself as a woman to help capture them? And you were part of the plan all along?"

"That's right," Kent said.

He looked as though he wanted to say more, but was scared to. Betty took a deep breath. This changed things, didn't it? Couldn't it? Kent hadn't been acting that way because of past temptations. He was...he was helping the town. Playing a role. And here, she'd thought the worst of him.

Betty bit her lip and stared at her shoes for a moment before bringing her eyes back up to his. Was there even an apology big enough for the one she owed him?

"I'm sorry I doubted you," she said.

"You had every reason to," Kent answered. "And I'm right proud of you for standing up for what you believe in. For having the courage to stay true to yourself and the things you believe in. Just...just wish I'd done that myself a long time ago."

"It can be hard," Betty said. "But you finally did. And that's all that matters." She gave a soft laugh. "I guess Sam was right after all. Well, half right, anyway."

"About what?" Kent asked. Then he scowled, "Can't imagine him being right about anything."

"He said I must be attracted to men with black pasts. At first, I got upset, but truthfully, I am attracted to a man who had a black past...one that he put behind him."

"I'm a little scared to ask," Kent said. "Does that mean you'll consider letting me call on you again?"

"I will," Betty said, smiling up at him. "There's nothing I'd like more."

"Then, I've got to tell you something," Kent said seriously.

Betty's smile faltered, and her heart started to thud in a worrying way. She pressed her hands to her stomach and swallowed hard. "What's that?"

"I'm awful fond of you, Betty, and once I start calling, I've the feeling it's not going to be long after that before I tell you how much I love you." Kent hesitated, then asked, "Are you okay with that?"

Her smile returned, and the tension Betty had been feeling slid off her shoulders. "More than okay," she said, stepping close, and rising on her tiptoes to press her lips to his.

Kent wrapped his arms around her, and Betty didn't care that they were in the street late at night and making a spectacle of themselves. She was overcome with relief. Her head rested against his chest, and for the first time in days, Betty felt safe, and protected, and—

"Betty?" Kent said.

She looked up at him. "What is it?"

"I can't wait any longer," Kent told her. "I love you.

Epilogue

Two months later

Kent walked toward Mrs. Stover's general store. He'd invited Betty and her aunt for dinner and offered to escort them. That morning, when he'd invited them, Mrs. Stover had made a big fuss over him, and how he'd protected Betty, and put a stop to the problems in town.

Truthfully, it had embarrassed him a little. After all, it was the gunslingers who had done most of the work. He'd just gone along with their plan. Besides, it had been some time ago. Still, he was relieved the woman liked and accepted him. At first, he hadn't been sure she would.

Someone was coming out of the general store, and Kent was surprised to see Gus, his shoulders slightly slumped. "Gus," he said. "How are you?"

"Right terrible," the old man admitted. "Been seeing some man hanging around the general store."

"Is that so?" Kent said. "You'd best act fast if you don't want to lose her."

"Lose who?" Gus asked, not meeting Kent's eye. "Don't know what you're talking about."

"Tell you what," Kent said. "Any night you want, you come to the restaurant for dinner with Mrs. Stover. On the house. It's the least I can do, you protecting Mrs. Stover and Betty while my hotel guests were causing trouble. I understand Mrs. Stover likes the special the chef makes on Thursdays."

"Does she?" Gus straightened a little. "I just might. See you later."

Kent watched as he left, feeling bad for Gus. Just as he was about to walk into the store, someone called his name. He turned to see Eli.

"Just need a moment of your time," the gunslinger said, walking over.

"What can I do for you?" Kent asked.

"There's a stagecoach coming in tomorrow. Got a wanted man on it," Eli said. "You up for helping us?"

"Me?" Kent asked. Surprise filled every inch of him.

"That's right," Eli said. "Could use another good man."

The words struck his chest like an arrow piercing through, and Kent fought for a moment to swallow down the emotion. A good man. It felt...well, it felt good hearing that.

"Just say when," Kent answered.

"We're meeting at the sheriff's office at nine in the morning," Eli said. He strode away calling, "See you there."

Feeling a little dazed, Kent walked into the general store. He walked up to the counter, and a silly grin spread across his face as he saw Betty. "You'll never believe what happened," he said.

"Tell me," she said.

"Eli Jones just asked me to help him and the others tomorrow on a job."

"Well, of course they did," Betty said, coming around the counter to give him a kiss. "They know a man they can count on when they see one."

"I'm just glad that all of them—and you—have forgiven and accepted me," Kent said.

"You've no idea how worried I was, seeing Sam here," Betty admitted.

"Did you hear anything yet, from your parents or sister?" Kent asked, leaning on the counter. "About Sam?"

Betty shook her head. "Only that the wedding was off. Mother didn't say why, and my sister hasn't written. Likely, she's embarrassed. Of course, I didn't tell them I knew what had happened. I wanted to focus on the good news in my letter, being with you." She laughed softly. "To think I was sad, at one point, that Sam had overlooked me. I sure saved myself a lot of trouble. And," she added, winking at Kent, "found a much better and better-looking beau."

"Got that right," Kent agreed. "I'm glad we moved here."

"So am I," Betty said softly. "This place was what we both needed. It brought us together. I couldn't ask for a better life than I have now."

"Are we ready?" Mrs. Stover asked, perching her hat on her head as she hurried toward them. "You are a dear boy, inviting this old lady along."

"It's my pleasure," Kent said.

As she locked the shop door, and they started walking toward the hotel, Kent realized he felt very differently than he had felt when he first moved to Red Ridge.

Pride. A sense of belonging.

Billy Madison passed by in a wagon, his wife Mirabelle with him. Both waved, and he returned the gesture. The local doctor and his wife were strolling along the street and said hello as they passed Kent.

"It feels good to be home," Kent said quietly. When Betty squeezed his arm, he knew she'd heard him. And he hoped when he asked her to marry him tonight, she'd say yes.

Betty might have thought she couldn't ask for anything better, but Kent planned to spend every minute of his life making sure hers was everything she could dream of.

***

Love is in the air for Gus, but what happens when the woman of his dreams has another man hanging around? One with poor intentions? Start reading *The Old Man now.*

***

Claim your bonus story!

When an old friend calls, legendary gunslingers Eli Jones, Billy Madison, and Gavin Jefferson answer without hesitation. They've faced down the toughest outlaws, always bringing justice with deadly precision and no remorse. But nothing could prepare them for the fiery Stella, a woman determined to blaze her own trail—even at risk to one of their own. Start reading *The Riders* now. You can also find the link at www.sarahlambbooks.com under "free book."

Read or Listen to the Red Ridge Chronicles Books

Amazon: https://www.amazon.com/dp/B0DQ7HFQ15
Audible:
https://www.audible.com/author/Sarah-Lamb/B098H3
SGLK

Book 1

The Gunslinger

Book 2

The Drifter

Book 3

The Lawman

Book 4

The Doctor

Book 5

The Tracker

Book 6

The Newcomer

Book 7

The Old Man

Book 8

The Christmas Wedding

Note from Author

Thank you for taking the time to read *The Newcomer*. Could I ask for one small favor? Reviews like yours on Amazon mean so much to me and help others to find my books! Even just a single line means a lot!

Also...

Want a FREE book?

Stop by my website to get your no strings attached **FREE book**. It's my gift to you, as a thank you for reading this one.

www.sarahlambbooks.com

About the Author

Sarah writes captivating characters and clean romance that's anything BUT boring! From heartbreaking moments to heartwarming tales, get swept away in either historical or small town romance that pulls you in until the last page.

Nestled in the Blue Ridge Mountains of Virginia where she's married to her Texan husband, you'll find Sarah creating her next book, spending time with her children, or volunteering in her community.

Want more of Sarah's books? Find them all on Amazon!

https://www.amazon.com/stores/Sarah-Lamb/author/B098H3SGLK

www.ingramcontent.com/pod-product-compliance
Lightning Source LLC
LaVergne TN
LVHW090948080826
845145LV00003B/935

* 9 7 8 1 9 6 0 4 1 8 6 3 0 *